ENOUGH IS ENOUGH

VOLUME 4

SUSAN KEENE

THE KATE NASH MYSTERIES

Publishing Coordinator – Sharon Kizziah-Holmes
Cover Design – Jaycee DeLorenzo

Published by Bent Willow Books
Niangua, MO

ISBN -13: 978-1-960499-18-9

In remembrance of
Nancy B. Dailey

Many thanks to Jennifer Birehmeier Darnell and Shirley McCann for their editing and proofreading on this book.

Thanks, also, to Sharon Kizziah-Holmes for her publishing coordinator expertise.

OTHER PUBLICATIONS BY SUSAN

CHAPTER 1

I looked around the room. Nothing special jumped out at me except the pictures of three men thumb tacked to a whiteboard. In a room like this, it meant the men had been murdered. Someone had made a murder board; the pictures of the victims would soon be joined by possible suspects and people of interest.

Amy Perkin, my business partner in the Nash and Perkin Detective Agency sat at one of the tables arranged in a U-shape. She tapped her fingers on the scarred and scratched surface in front of her. At the end sat my hubby, Ryan Meade. He had his phone to his ear, giving directions to someone on the other end of the line. He nodded at me in greeting and went back to his call. I took a seat between them.

I couldn't fathom why my old partner, Roger Simon, from St. Louis Homicide wanted us to meet him in one of the conference rooms at the police station. We sat quietly, except for Ryan's muffled voice on the phone, the room was silent.

He kept us twiddling our thumbs for over twenty

minutes. It wasn't something Roger Simon did. For ten years he and I had each other's backs during some horrendous situations. But it had been a few years since I sat in front of a murder board.

Ryan, my friend of many years and my husband of a few months, owned a world-wide security company and had nothing to do with the police except for the times they used our equipment. Ours was state of the art and out worked anything the force could offer to solve their cases. Only the initialed national and international law enforcement groups had anything newer or better.

We all looked up when the door on the other side of the room opened. Roger walked in with such an armload of files, he had to reach back and close the door with his foot. He let the folders fall onto the tabletop.

His suit looked slept in, he had a stubble on his chin and his eyes were bloodshot. He let out a deep breath. "Thanks for coming," he said. "I'll get right to the point. In the last month we have had three bold, in the public's eye, murders. We have no clues and no suspects."

"And this affects us how?" Ryan asked. Even though his words were harsh, his tone stayed friendly and even.

"I need to hire the three of you to help me out with this case. At one murder scene, bystanders saw a well-dressed woman walk out of the building, where a shooting took place, drop a gun in a grate in the sidewalk, get into the back seat of a white limo with black tinted windows, and drive away. That was three weeks ago. Although there were at least fifty people in the area when the crime went down, we have only a vague description of the killer, the car and the driver. It doesn't seem possible.

"At the second crime scene, a lady, and I use the term loosely, walked out of the Winter Oaks Bar after she shot a man six times, dropped a gun down a street grate, got into a white limo and drove away. Again, no one saw the woman when she went into the bar. If they did, they didn't notice her. She is smart enough to know everyone would look at the gun, fearing for their own safety. No one could give any details about the woman."

Amy started to say something, Roger lifted his arm with his hand in a stop position and said, "It doesn't end there. At the third murder, just three days ago, a woman got out of a car in front of St. Paul's Episcopal Church, where a wedding was in progress. She walked up the stairs, went into the church, shot a man as he sat in the back row, dropped the gun onto the pew next to him and walked out. She calmly got into the back of a limo and drove off.

"Let me read to you the witness statements of some of the people who saw the suspect as she fled the scenes."

I put my hand up in a halt gesture, as he had done earlier, but I didn't let him stop me from speaking. "This is all very interesting. Thing is, it has nothing to do with the three of us. I doubt the big brass upstairs, and at city hall, would let you hire outsiders to solve the case. I, above all, know how protective they are of their work, their money and their reputation."

Roger, who had been standing, pulled out the chair in front of him. He moved around in front of it and nearly fell into the seat. I'd never seen him look as defeated as he did right then.

"Let me start at the beginning. I need to hire the three of you to help with the murders I just told you about. Due to the pandemic, we have one vice cop, two in burglary and about forty percent of the beat and traffic cops we need to keep this town relatively safe. Every day one comes back and two more are out sick. Covid, and fear of covid, is eating our staff up.

"Those who are here are not thrilled to go out on the streets and confront people they know haven't seen a doctor in years, much less had a vaccination," he finished.

"Roger, do you realize what you just said? You want us to go out and confront people because your folks don't want to because of the pandemic," I said.

"I guess I could have put it a gentler way. Sorry, I'm frustrated. I'm tired of the whining about having to wear a mask, infringing on rights because they don't want the vaccine, yet they won't do either.

"Some are dying, some are only sick, and no one is around to handle this murder case."

Ryan still had his phone in his hand. He put it back to his ear and said, "I'll have to call you later." He turned his attention back to Roger. "And you are certain the three of us can solve the case and stay well, when your crew can't or won't. In what capacity do you want to hire us?"

Roger stood, rested both palms of his hands on the table and leaned forward with his elbows locked. He looked us in the eye, one at a time. "I need to swear you all in as detectives with the rank of Lieutenant. Everyone has signed off on it all the way to the top. We are desperate." He walked over to the murder board behind him and pinned up three more photos. He pointed to them.

The photos were of women, or one woman who could change the way she walked and stood. She didn't look as if she was trying to hide. She was the kind of lady you turned around and took another look at. All the photos showed the suspect to have perfect posture. She stood around five feet ten with heels. It could have been the same woman or three separate ones. The other pictures were of the dead men.

He pointed out each of the women wore a long dress, a loose blazer, gold hooped earrings, white gloves and spike-heeled shoes. All of the pictures were profiles. In this day and age when everyone grabbed a cellphone to memorialize the events of the day, it looked as if these photos were taken by traffic cameras at nearby intersections.

There were several pictures of a white stretch limousine with a clear picture of the license plates with ENUFSENUF. The plate looked real but was issued by the *State of Confusion*.

Ryan looked at me and I glanced toward Amy. I knew she and I weren't going to say *no* but I couldn't read Ryan's face. Even if he wanted to join in, I doubted he could. One of his accounts entailed security for the St. Louis Cardinals and we were in the middle of the season. He owned four restaurants, an art gallery, and had accounts in every state, along with most European and peaceful South American countries.

"I miss my days as a cop," Amy said. "I'm willing. And I don't think social distancing will be a problem. It's been eighteen months. We have had all the shots and boosters. I don't wear a mask anymore unless they are by the front door when I enter an establishment.

Most people have done what they intend to do to protect themselves."

"You know me," I added. "I like a good mystery."

We all looked at Ryan. "Sorry Roger. I'm just too busy and either one of these women can investigate circles around me. I don't have any trips planned and I can consult, but it is about all the time I can spare. As a matter of fact, I am extremely late for a meeting. I wish you the best of luck." He stood, walked over to Roger, shook his hand and nodded at Amy and me before he walked out.

Roger left the room and came immediately back holding two sets of credentials and the papers we needed to sign after we took the oath to protect and serve.

"I have cars waiting outside. They are equipped with all the standard gadgets and are unmarked."

Roger looked five years younger than he did when we first saw him. "Let me tell you what I know. Then you can work here or at your place or both."

Amy took a small notebook out of her blazer and a pen from her pants pocket. I laid my phone on the table and turned it on record.

Roger began.   "This woman walked into the Samuelson Building, downtown. She took the elevator to the fifth floor, sat quietly as she waited about five minutes to get in to see Marcus Dames. She shot him twice in the chest and once in the head.

"No one heard the shots. There was no sign of a silencer at the scene. According to witnesses, she took the stairs to the garage where a white limo waited for her. She got in the back seat, and it drove off turning left toward Kings Highway. One traffic camera caught it a couple of blocks away and then it disappeared, as did the woman. The windows on the car were too dark for the driver to be seen.

"Even though we have found all three guns, they are pristine. They have no serial numbers. They have had the barrels roughed up so the identification of the spent shells is impossible. I don't know how they do it. There is no time to manipulate the gun between when the women or woman drops the weapon and when the crime lab picks it up, but there are no fingerprints or identifying marks what-so-ever."

"In the first murder, the weapon was a 38 revolver. The next one we recovered shell casings and bullets from the victim, it was a 9 mm. Like I said, the guns looked like a hot poker or a drill bit had been run through them so, no help there.

"The third man, the guy at the wedding, was killed with a 22. She emptied the gun into him. You know how big that place is. The wedding probably had five hundred plus guests and the noise level was high."

Roger straightened the folders in front of him. "Do you want to hear more about the killer or killers?"

Amy stood and began to take the pictures down from the murder board. "We will do better if we begin this investigation at the beginning. We will talk to the witnesses, review the crime scenes ourselves, and we'll get back to you when we know something.

"Feel free to check in with us whenever you want. I'm sure the top brass will be hounding you every day for news."

Roger smiled for the first time all day. "I'm sure they will. I'll keep them out of your hair as best I can.

"Right now, we have no women in homicide, and

even though we have three coming out of training soon, none of them could hold a candle to you. Whoever is killing these men has a reason. I don't have the resources right now to figure out what the dead men have in common.

"No one takes the chances these people are taking if they don't have a good reason. They have got to have connections to get the weapons. They are well dressed, have money and are well- organized. I believe them to be different heights and weights, but witnesses describe them all the same."

"The only fact we know is the same in all three murders is the car. It is a stretch limo with the vanity license plate, *ENUFSENUF.*

"They seem to have a sense of humor, State of Confusion. The plate is red with white lettering.

"I need women who can infiltrate spas, bars, PTA meetings and such, and their presence will not be questioned."

Amy and I looked at one another. "You can quit with the hard sell," I said. "We will figure it out. Can you have someone put all of the files in my car? And, we don't need cars. We will take mine. I would like to have a police radio for each of us in case we need you right away."

CHAPTER 2

Once Amy and I were in the car alone, we began to talk. "What do you think?" I asked.

"The entire situation or the murders?" She answered.

"That's a strange answer." I didn't want to push.

"This case is my first attempt to be normal since we lost the baby. It feels wrong," she said. "Do you think it's wrong?"

I had started the SUV. I shut it off and turned toward her. "Not at all. We have all been worried about you. There was nothing you could have done differently. I've never lost a baby, but I lost Michael after six years of a beautiful marriage. I felt the same way you do now. It took a long time before I made the decision to move on and date Ryan."

"In my heart, I know you're right. Be patient with me." She gave me a slight smile.

I put my hand on her shoulder. "Always, always."

The rest of the ride home was quiet until my cell phone rang. I turned it on from the steering wheel and put it on the speaker. "Hello?"

Ryan's voice came through the radio. "Is Amy still with you? Nathan and I just finished troubleshooting a problem at the stadium. We are only a few blocks from Peacemaker. Thought you two might want to meet us for dinner."

Amy answered. "Sure, but what about the dogs? They will have their legs crossed by the time we get home if they have to wait to go outside."

Nathan spoke up. "We dropped by both places and let them out before our last appointment. They have even been fed. I'm craving oysters."

"Okay, see you there," I said before we hung up.

Amy looked my way. "I'm excited to get started on the murder case."

"I am too. I'm so tired of background checks. Hopefully Ryan will turn the chore over to his guys again and we won't get behind."

She raised both hands and had her fingers crossed on both of them. "Besides, I've been hungry for something good, but I didn't know what. As soon as I heard the name of the restaurant, I knew I craved a shrimp po boy."

I chuckled. "I'm going for a lobster, a Caesar salad and a baked potato with butter, sour cream, chives and cheese."

"Kate, it has always amazed me you can eat like that and never gain any weight."

"Look who's talking. What are you, five feet ten and one hundred and twenty pounds? I swear, you could hide sideways behind a telephone pole."

We arrived at the café ten minutes later and the guys were waiting in the parking lot. They got out of Ryan's truck and walked toward my car. "We're looking for a couple of women of the evening, are you ladies game?"

We both laughed and said, "always for you," at the same time.

Ryan had made reservations and we were seated in a quiet corner near the back. The layout made each and every booth a private space except for four tables in the front. We ordered appetizers of calamari, lobster bites, fried cheese and spinach and artichoke dip.

Amy and I had a glass of wine in front of us and the guys had a beer. The waiter served our appetizers and we began to banter pleasantly when we heard a commotion toward the front of the house.

I put my new badge on the band of my slacks, drew my Glock 42 and headed in that direction. I could feel Amy behind me. We stopped abruptly when we heard gunshots, five of them. Someone yelled, "Call the police!"

"We are the police," I said as I came upon the scene. A man lay forward with his head resting in his dinner plate and three obvious holes in the back of his head.

Amy walked toward the front door. "What happened here?"

"I'm not sure," the hostess said, "a woman came in, I asked her if I could seat her, and she answered she would only be a minute. She walked over to that table, shot that guest and dropped a gun on the floor. She looked back at me and said thank you. She calmly walked out the door and that was it."

Amy and I ran outside. Ryan and Nathan, who both had conceal and carry permits were behind us. Ryan walked to the front door. "No one is to leave this building," he said in an authoritative voice. He turned to Nathan. "Go in the back and make sure no one leaves."

The young man who worked the valet parking area had little to say. Amy wrote down his name, Aaron White. "A white limo drove up. A woman got out and went into the restaurant. In less than a minute she came back out, handed me a twenty dollar bill, and said thank you. She opened the back door of the limo and climbed in. They drove off."

"What's your name?" I asked the second boy. I say boy because I doubt he was over twenty years old.

"Warren, Warren James. I didn't see anything though. I was at the door with the Bange family. They are elderly and frail, and we always take them inside."

"Do the Banges come here often?"

"Yes. They are here every Friday night. They always come to eat the fish. They say this is the best in the city."

Now both young men were standing next to one another. "Aaron, you saw and spoke to the woman who got into the limousine?" I asked.

"Yes, but I can't tell you anything about her. She had on a thick vail and white gloves."

Amy asked, "did she speak to you?

"Yes," he answered. "She sounded old."

I jumped on his comment. "Why do you say that?"

"I don't know. I talk to lots of people every night. You can tell an old person from a young person from their voice. You know, kind of shaky, and lower than a young voice."

Amy and I shared a glance. She spoke to both boys. "This is a crime scene. Don't give anyone their car unless we say it is okay. No one leaves, got it?"

"There was one more thing I just thought of. The killer was left handed. I know by the way she handed me the money. She also had a watch on her right wrist."

"You're very observant, Aaron. What did the watch look like?"

"I believe it was a superhero. A kid's watch. I couldn't tell you who it was. It was small and she wore it with the face down."

"Yes, detective, the more you remember, the bigger the tips."

"Remember," Amy said, "no one leaves.

CHAPTER 3

Amy and I neither one had stopped by the table where the dead man sat slumped over with his head on the table on our way out the door. Blood ran down the back of his neck. I knew the front of his head would no longer be there. We didn't touch him; too many traumatized people eating while the killing went down and we didn't need to add more gruesome images to what they had already witnessed. I knew by the looks on the faces of those around me, it might be a long time before they rested comfortably at night. Some would never sleep again if they saw his brains in his salmon, which I knew they were.

It didn't take a coroner to know the man died instantly. He had one bullet hole at the base of his neck which would have severed his brainstem. The second shot had entered his left temple and the third had hit him in the back just above where the top of the chair would have hit him.

"I called an ambulance, Roger, and the crime scene crew," Ryan said. "Everyone is on the way."

I looked around the room. The diners and wait staff were still, each and every person in the restaurant had fear in his eyes. Plates full of food sat untouched. Men held on to their wives and parents to their children.

A woman in a wheelchair rolled up next to the dead man. She stared at him, unblinking, obviously in shock. The other two people in the foursome leaned against the nearest wall. Both of them had blood splatter on their hands and clothes, and the man had it on his face. He, too, didn't take his eyes off the dead man.

The customers in the dining room, who sat close enough to see the killing, were no help. They had either heard the gunshots and ducked down in their seats or booths, or they only saw the gun. The best description we were able to put together of the shooter was a well-dressed woman who wore a hat, gloves, and something over her face.

She walked in and three shots rang out. She turned and walked out as calmly as she came in. Ninety percent of the people who sat close to the front of the dining room didn't even notice she dropped the gun.

Roger Simon showed up with the CSI team, but he didn't step in and take over. He couldn't believe we happened to be eating in the same restaurant where another murder took place.

Neither could I. Not only would the news of the murder be front page news, but once again, I'd be in the spotlight.

There were eighty-three people at various points in their dinner when the killing went down. Some, like the four of us, were enjoying their first course, while others had been finishing up. We questioned each of them.

Three hours after we arrived, we had everyone's

name, address and contact information. The victim's name was Victor Mann, a sixty-three-year-old man who owned a furniture store in O'Fallon. Mann seemed to be a creature of habit. He would be easy to track down since he drove thirty miles with his wife and business partner to have dinner at the same restaurant every Friday.

According to both his wife and partner, he ran a lucrative business. He didn't cheat people with his products. He'd been married to Mariam for thirty-three years, had three grown children, two of whom worked at the store and one who lived in Miami.

On the surface, he seemed completely benign. Of course we would even know what kind of toothpaste he used by the time we were done investigating him.

After speaking with everyone, we knew exactly what the woman did when she arrived. She drove up in a white limo, got out by herself, walked into the establishment, shot and killed one person. She dropped the gun, a .22, on the floor, walked calmly out the door and left in the same car.

Ellen Wycoff, the hostess, said her voice had the same timbre as someone who had laryngitis.

The red license plate had white lettering, ENUFSENUF.

As Aaron told us matter-of-factly, ENUFSENUF Issued by *The State of Confusion*.

I told Ryan, "Someone has a sense of humor."

CHAPTER 4

Mariam Mann told us she had no idea who had shot her husband nor did she know anyone who would want him dead. She'd been in a wheelchair for the better part of a year due to recuring blood clots in her legs.

Mann Furniture had been recognized three years in a row as the most popular business in O'Fallon. It made Kate believe the reason for the killings had nothing to do with cheating or bad business.

The Mann's lived in Lake St. Louis. His business partner, when we talked about it later, we believed to be more distraught than the dead man's wife. Some of that could have been attributed to the blood spatter he had on his face and clothes. Once we finished questioning them, we let the partners, Ethel and Raymond Burke, use the restrooms to clean up and let them leave.

We called Mrs. Mann's daughter in Ladue and had a cab take the poor lady to her house. We had offered her a ride in a squad car but she understandably refused.

Ryan and Nathan weren't shy about questioning the

rest of the diners. By the time the CSI team finished with the crime scene, they had seen every patron, had names, addresses, and initial impressions for each of them.

The restaurant owner, Edward Well, said he knew the Manns. They had been coming in for their favorite dishes for over ten years. He said anyone who knew them well would know they were guests every Friday night and had a reserved table at the front of the dining room due to the "missus and her wheelchair".

He took it well when we told him he couldn't open the café for a few days. Even though the crime took place practically right inside the front door, the entire place would be gone over with a fine-tooth comb again before he could clean and open for business.

At well after midnight, we left the crime scene and headed toward Amy and Nathan's place.

Nathan, who sat in the backseat with Amy, leaned forward and suggested we stop for food since we had not gotten to eat.

"I had my heart set on a po boy, but I'll settle for an order of sweet 'n sour chicken from the Chinese Palace," Amy said.

We all agreed and picked up enough food for an army and took it to Amy's house. Instead of dropping them off, Ryan and I went in with them and ate our dinner at nearly one a.m.

"What do you think?" Ryan asked. "Whoever she or they are, they have nerves of steel. It takes a gutsy person to walk into a crowded restaurant, shoot a gun, and walk out like you just bought a loaf of bread."

I took a bite of a crab Rangoon. "I don't remember seeing a veil on the woman in the pictures Roger gave us. The valet said she had on a thick veil and he couldn't see her features. Him seeing a watch on her right wrist was a plus. We need to look at the pictures again. We must have missed it."

Amy added, "Everyone who sees the white limo can tell us about it. She is careful about the details of the murders yet she comes and goes in a conspicuous white stretch limo with a driver and a license plate no one forgets. I think we should try to find the car."

"It might be difficult. All of the killings take place in high traffic areas, and Roger said they always see her on the first camera and then the car doesn't show up again," I said.

Ryan stood. "You ladies will have to take this up again in the morning. I have an early meeting, and Nathan has to supervise an installation at three auto repair shops." He leaned over, kissed Amy on the cheek, shook Nathan's hand and we left.

"I hate to bring this up, but Amy left her truck, and my car is still at the restaurant."

He nodded toward the garage door. "Amy's car is in the garage and yours is sitting in our driveway. I sent a couple of the guys to take care of it."

"How did they get the keys?" I asked.

He shrugged, gave a little chuckle and said, "Surely you jest."

CHAPTER 5

We didn't arrive home until after three a.m. As we opened the kitchen door both dogs were waiting for us. Axel, our German Shepard being the gentleman he always was, sat quietly and waited for us to give him a command to come to one of us. Chili, on the other hand, my miniature dachshund, barked, ran in circles and jumped in front of one of us and then the other.

I reached down to pick her up. She wiggled and squirmed to get to Ryan and once he had her, she wiggled and squirmed to get back to me. Such is the nature of her breed.

Ryan gave me Chili as a gift. I loved her dearly. Axel, we bought because some of our cases not only put me and Amy in danger, but also our families. Axel, a military trained dog, watches the house, Ryan and me and Chili.

Before Axel, we would have had to walk Chili no matter what hour we came in because she had a way of getting into trouble in the yard alone. Twice someone tried to take her. We walk both dogs morning and night, except on occasions such as this when it was too late to walk them or we were too tired. I opened the screen door and they both ran out. Axel ran around the edge of the fence and barked once; his signal to Chili, who had been waiting on the porch, that it was safe for her to come into the yard.

They were fun to watch. Axel played with his little sister, but he also acted as a babysitter.

Within a few minutes they were back inside and we all went up to bed. Chili slept with Ryan and me. Axel slept in her bed on the floor near the bedroom door where she could best protect her family.

I wanted to talk to Ryan about the case, but by the time I came out of the bathroom I could tell from his breathing, he was asleep.

A few hours later, a small happy ray of sunshine hit my pillow. I stretched, yawned and sat on the edge of the bed. I couldn't find Chili under the covers. When I glanced at the clock, I knew why. I slept until nine-fifteen.

The smell of coffee floated up the stairs along with Amy and Ryan's voices speaking in low tones. I went to the bathroom, took a quick shower and slipped on a pair of ragged jeans and a faded St. Louis Cardinal's tee shirt. One of the perks of having the office in the house, I didn't have to dress up every day.

"You two are chatty. Have you solved the murders?" I said as I came down the stairs.

"No," Amy said, "but I have a skinny latte for you, blueberry bagels and the cream cheese is softening on the counter."

As I passed Ryan, I kissed him lightly on the cheek.

"Why didn't you wake me up this morning?"

"You looked so peaceful," he said. "I need to leave. My meeting is in Troy."

Amy handed him a go-cup full of coffee. "That's a long drive."

"I don't mind. It's a beautiful day. I'll check in later and see if you two learned anything new." He turned around to the dogs, petted each of them and said, "Keep your mother safe today." On his way out the door, he turned back. "Where are Sally and Digger?"

"At the groomers. Nathan will pick them up between jobs today and bring them here." At the same time we bought Axel, Amy and Nathan fell in love with a Rottweiler named Sally. None of us had to worry about anyone breaking and entering with Sally or Axel on duty.

"Where do you want to start?" I asked Amy.

"I thought we should go to the crime scenes. Sometimes, with a little prodding, people remember more than they think they do."

"Sounds good. Guess we should leave the dogs here. It is too hot to leave them in the car in this weather."

I took a closer look at Amy . She wore a pair of pale green Alice + Olivia wide leg slacks in black leather, black Clark scuffs and a beige Lilysilk blouse. Around her neck hung a two inch circular moonstone pendant sitting in a crescent moon. She was truly beautiful. I thought so the first time I met her ten years ago and, if anything, she grew more gorgeous as the years passed.

Her twenty-four inch waist, modest breasts, jet black hair and long legs caused people, especially men, to take a second look.

I had on the ragged jeans and faded tee shirt I put on

in the morning. "Give me five minutes to change. By the way, where is your gun?"

She grinned at me which showed off her perfectly straight and sparkling white teeth. "It's in the car. Since we are playing cops, I don't have to conceal it. I intend to wear it in a holster on my hip."

It took me less than five minutes to change. Unlike Amy who stood five-feet-ten, I stood five-four in the spike heels I wore everywhere. My standard outfit consisted of a pair of men's tailored slacks, a blouse of some sort, and a blazer to hide the 9 mm I wore in a shoulder holster.

After brushing my curly and unruly hair, I lassoed it into a low ponytail and bounced back downstairs.

I liked Amy's idea to wear my gun on the outside. Nothing about me shouted, big and strong. My biggest pet peeve was when someone called me *little lady*.

Amy called the dogs to her one at a time and talked to them like they were children who were told they couldn't go to a birthday party. "We'll be back soon."

CHAPTER 6

One of the shootings took place in an office building in downtown St. Louis. To me it seemed the most puzzling. The killer rode in an elevator to the fifth floor, sat in a waiting room for several minutes and when she finally got to Dennis Small's office, she shot him three times at close range.

Amy read the police report Roger Simon gave us about the murder while I drove. "From the crime scene investigation, it sounded like Small opened the door to the killer. The killer didn't take the time to step in. She shot him two times in the chest, once in the head and left.

"What does that sound like?" I asked. Before Amy could answer, I continued. "It sounds like someone who had conceal and carry classes." First, they ask you if you are sure you could take a person's life if you were in a him or me situation. If you say *no*, they tell you to go on home. Before the class is over, they let you know the best way to make sure the perp isn't going to get up and hurt you is two shots to the chest and one to the head.

Amy glanced up from the notes, looked my way and said, "According to this, she killed most everyone the same way, two to the chest and one to the head. Of course we don't know which shot came first."

"Back to Dennis Small," I said, "no one heard strange noises or shots being fired. The girl at the reception counter said she didn't see the woman leave. She could have been away from her desk or transcribing something with her headphones on. She might even have been a part of it."

I took a sip of the latte I had with me. "What did she say about the woman's appearance? Her statement says she told the lady to take a seat until Mr. Small could see her."

"She didn't say much. She remembered the woman as stately. That word always unnerves me. Exactly what does stately mean? Was she tall and thin or did she merely stand up straight?"

"I don't know Kate, but we will have to interview her at her house. She has been having panic attacks since the killing of her boss and quit her job."

"Or maybe she had a guilty conscience because of her part in killing him," I said.

The building looked like every other office building in the heart of the city. You could see little as you drove down the street. The avenues were narrow, the buildings too tall to let any sun in except at high noon when it shined straight down and made the area feel like a sauna.

"What do you notice first?" Amy asked.

"That the streets are too narrow for a big limo to sit double parked out front without causing at least one person a problem."

"Exactly. I bet a delivery driver, or a client in a hurry or maybe a cop told the driver to move."

Amy made a note.

The nearest parking garage was a three block walk to the east. There were back doors and underground walkways for the people who worked in the buildings, but we suckers who had business with one of the lawyers, real estate magnates, tax accountants or investment firms had to hoof the three blocks back to the building from the parking garage.

There were two or three buildings with an awning, but they were barely wide enough for one person to take cover from the weather.

On the menu near a bank of elevators, a sign had all of the offices listed according to profession. Under "Financial Advisors", we found the name; Dennis Small, fifth floor, suite three.

The elevator stopped on the fifth floor but no one occupied the reception desk. We walked on until we found suite three. We heard nothing, no talking, no doors opening and closing, and no more elevator noise after we got off. I wondered if the entire floor had shut down.

The crime scene had been cleaned up. Nothing was locked. The office, except for the blood stains near the door, looked as if the occupant stepped out to use the bathroom and would be back any minute.

We walked in. "Let's see if they missed anything. I'll take the desk," I said to Amy, "you take the file cabinet."

His desk had nothing of value in it. Pictures of what I thought must be his family sat on the shelves of a bookcase. Several pictures of a pretty woman, he held possessively, sat on his desk. The picture sat separated from the others. The frame looked old and the child's clothes didn't look modern. I took a picture of it with my phone.

When we were done, we sat on the couch across from the desk. The position of it would have made it impossible for whoever sat on it to see the person sitting at the desk on a sunny day. The afternoon glare blocked everything. We took pictures of the room including the blood on the floor and the blood spatter on the walls and the desk.

If there were clues to who shot Dennis Small and why, they were not in his office.

CHAPTER 7

On the way out of the building, we stopped at the main desk on the first floor and talked to the receptionist for the entire building. She remembered the woman who came in and asked to see Dennis Small.

She described her at about five-five, but she didn't know what kind of shoes she had on. "Heels are what a woman would usually wear with a dress as fancy as she wore."

We leaned against a tall semi-circular wooden partition she sat behind. "Why didn't you tell the police what you knew about the woman?"

She looked down and away from us. "I didn't know she killed anybody. The police ushered us all into a conference room, took our names and addresses and told us we could leave. There wasn't much of a police presence either. A tall guy in a suit, three patrolmen and an ambulance crew. The coroner came in and about twenty minutes later they took the body out."

Amy asked, "What's your name?"

"James, April James."

"Close your eyes. Try to picture every detail of what happened and what you saw from the time the woman walked into the building and left again," Amy said.

"Like I said, she was about five feet five. Her hair and dress were white. Her make-up was way too light for her, and her eyebrows were drawn on with a high arch, like a cartoon character. She wore bright purple lipstick and walked with a limp." She stood up and shifted from her left foot to her right. "She favored her right leg," she said.

I said, "In order to see Mr. Small she must have had an appointment, is that correct?"

"Yes, that's correct. She said her name was Audrey Hepburn."

Amy smiled. "And you didn't think that was a bit odd?"

"No, why?"

"No reason," Amy said.

"Anything else?" I asked.

"No. Marsha Rains, Mr. Small's assistant called down and said she could come up, so I sent her."

"Do you know where Miss Rains was while her boss got murdered."

"No, it was her first day. I met her when she came in, and I never saw her again. I assumed she didn't like the job considering what happened and never came back."

Amy and I looked at one another.

"One more thing," I asked. "Did you see a white limo outside, double parked?"

"Yes, Miss Hepburn got in it and it drove away."

We started to leave when I had a thought and I

turned around and asked, "did Audrey Hepburn have an accent?"

"Oh, yes, it was Hispanic. It's why I thought her make-up was too light. It didn't match her dark complexion. I thought maybe she didn't know what color to use."

Amy and I looked at one another. With help like what we got from Miss James, there might be a little hope after all.

CHAPTER 8

As we left the building, I noticed a doorman. He wasn't the one we passed when we went into the building. "Sir," I said, "several days ago, when Mr. Small was shot to death upstairs, were you on duty?"

"Yes and no," he answered.

Amy and I looked at one another. She asked, "were you standing out here when a white limousine drove up, a lady got out and went into the building?"

"I was here when she left, but not when she came."

"Where were you when the woman went into the building?" Amy continued.

"I must have been down at the corner getting coffee. They don't care if I have coffee and set it on the stairs there." He turned around and pointed to a paper cup he had sitting behind the door and nearly out of sight.

"So what did you do when you came back and saw the limo double parked?"

"Nothing. It happens all the time. Three blocks is too far for some of the folks to walk so someone lets them out. The driver either sits and waits; or drives around the block until their passenger comes out."

"What did the driver of the car look like?"

"Oh, officer," he said to me, "the windows of the car were so dark, I couldn't see in and I remember wondering if it was legal to have them tinted so dark."

"How long was the car parked there?"

"I'm not certain. It was there when I came back with my coffee. Then a lady came through the door, dropped a gun down that grate behind you, got into the back seat and the car drove away."

"Which way did they go?"

He smiled a sheepish grin. "You can only go east, Miss. It's a one-way street."

I looked up at the corners of the buildings and over the doors but saw no cameras. "Do you have cameras?"

"No, nothing here to steal. Just a bunch of uppity men and women in fancy clothes and expensive shoes either making or losing money for one another."

Amy took a card from her pocket and gave it to the man. "If you think of anything else, call us." We started to walk away and Amy looked back. "How did you know the woman dropped a gun down the grate? How did you know it wasn't a phone or a wallet?"

"Because she made it a point to show the gun to me before she let go of it. I think she was trying to scare me. Did anybody tell you about the tattoo on her right hand?"

"No, no, they didn't. You tell me about it," I said.

"It was a broken heart. You know, a red heart with a jagged line through it."

"How big was it?" Amy asked.

"Tiny. She had on long sleeves but when she held

the gun out for me to see, her sleeve went up. I noticed it because it was such an odd color. The top half was bright red and the bottom a lighter color; I guess you'd call it pink. She had hairy arms. Most women don't have hair all the way down on the wrist like she did."

I asked, "did she have the gun in her right hand or her left."

"Left," he said.

"You sound pretty certain."

"I am. The grate is right down there." He pointed to his left. I could see it clearly. "She stopped, showed me the gun and then dropped it. At that time she only held it with her thumb and fore-finger. She definitely had it in her right hand when she let go of it. Of course, at that time, I didn't know she had shot Mr. Small, so I wasn't sure the gun was real. There are some strange people around here."

"Did she say anything else?" Amy asked.

"Yes, she handed me a twenty dollar bill and told me to have a nice day."

"Did she have an accent?"

"No."

CHAPTER 9

Amy and I walked back to the car in silence. Once we got there, she said., "Let's go back to the office and see if there is anyone in one of the databases with a tattoo of a broken heart in red and pink."

"I'd like to go by the church first. It's only a few blocks. I'm encouraged that we have two clues, aren't you?"

"It beats a poke in the eye with a sharp stick." I winked at her.

St. Paul's Episcopal Church was built in 1899. If it weren't for the Arch, the church steeple would have been the tallest structure in St. Louis. The building took up an entire city block. I counted eighteen stairs to get to the first landing. They were nearly twenty feet wide and there were at least three feet between steps. The average step height is around seven inches. I'd say these were at least nine inches deep. The landing measured about thirty feet, and then there were four more steps leading up to a smaller landing in front of the main door.

To run down the steps would have been dangerous. You'd have to step down, take three or four steps and step down again. At the landing it would be step down, take 20 steps, step down again.

I looked to my left and saw a concrete ramp from the top of the upper landing all the way to the sidewalk by the street. No one had said they saw her on the steps or on the ramp. "Amy, did it say anywhere in the notes Roger gave us there were any cameras around?"

"No, but it would be odd for there not to be cameras on one of the premier landmarks of the area," she said.

I turned around and looked back down to the street where we left my car with a red light spinning on the dashboard, and a sign at the top of the windshield saying, "Police", so it wouldn't get towed away. "How would you do coming up those stairs, going in, shooting someone a few times and then quickly managing your way down before someone came after you?"

She said, "I would take the ramp. I bet she did and didn't hurry."

Amy continued. "I figure human nature would be to check the person who she shot. He sat in the back row. She had to have tossed the gun since it landed two pews up on the other side. This place is so big and the music was still playing. But not many people heard the shots. Those who saw something wrong, ran to the injured man."

"You're probably right," I said. "How did the bride and groom leave the church?"

I looked up to watch Amy as she studied the area. "It says here in the report they were supposed to leave the church in a horse and buggy. They were to ride to

Union Station, get in their car and meet at the Adam's Mark. Let's talk to the carriage driver and ask if he got a good look at her. Do you have his name? I am sure their plans didn't follow their timeline after the shooting."

Amy looked at her notes. "The horses are housed in East Carondelet and taxied back and forth when they are needed. A note here says a group is trying its best to ban the horse buggy because it's cruel to the animals. A police sergeant by the name of Ranse Germaine said he ran into protesters when he went to interview the driver.

"We passed East Carondelet when we were looking for who we thought was Lizzy Smith's abductor. It's only about ten miles. Let's go take a look."

"Anyone else you want to talk to here at the church?" She asked.

"No, the reports I read said no one saw the murder. I think our best bet is the driver."

The driver wasn't at the stables. The caretaker told us he'd retired after thirty-one years. He assured us the only thing the man mentioned was the limousine. We were told he noticed it because it took the exact space the carriage should have had. The driver, a Mr. Reedy Smith, told his boss he would not have noticed it but he thought maybe he was at the wrong church. He was about to call the boss when a woman in white came out of the church, skipped rapidly down the stairs and got into the limo in question.

"That's one question answered," I said. "We know she took the stairs. And now we know she's athletic."

Reedy appeared, according to the report, to be more worried about getting his job done correctly than the woman or the limo.

On our way back to St. Louis, we stopped by a local

fast food drive-in. We each got a burger, onion rings and a Pepsi. At a roadside park, we pulled over, ate our lunch and talked about what we knew so far. Nothing.

CHAPTER 10

At two-thirty, we parked in the lot of the White Oaks Bar in Harvester. Harvester, St. Charles, St. Peters and O'Fallon used to be separate cities with a few miles in between. In the past twenty years, the area has grown so much they run into each other. If you go west, across the Interstate Seventy bridge, you are in St. Louis County.

The White Oaks Bar sat at the edge of where four upper-middle class neighborhoods came together. The tavern had a private lot on both sides of the building. We parked the car and went inside.

The space looked clean and neat. The decorations were 60's black and white pictures of the era. There were three pool tables and four dart boards set up for, what looked like, dart tournaments.

A bar ran across the entire back wall of the place, and at the end were round tables with plaid cloths and chairs with leather seats in red, blue, yellow and green. I could see myself hanging out there.

What I couldn't see, the way the bar ran and the fact

the dining area took up the back and the noisy games that were by the door, was how anyone could walk in, shoot someone six times and get out without anyone stopping them.

Our notes told us the owner's name, Wayne Barstone, a great name for a tavern owner, and the manager's name, Tiffany Majors. They were serving the few customers at the bar. She smiled at us when we came in. "Have a seat, ladies. Someone will be right with you."

I liked Tiffany right away. She was one of the few women I met who matched me in height. Her dishwater-blond hair hung in a ponytail down her back. Under her low cut top she wore a push up bra. No one had to look down her blouse, the girls were there for all to see. I have no idea how she fit into the jeans she wore.

Although she only stood about five-feet one and couldn't weigh more than a hundred and ten pounds, the jeans still looked painted on. She wore a short apron around her waist and a broad smile on her face. I wouldn't call her pretty, but appealing and approachable both came to mind.

When we stood by the bar and didn't move toward a table, she finished serving the man in front of her and walked toward us. "Can I help you gals?"

We both pointed to the badges on our belts, and I said, "Police."

The smile never left her face. Amy asked, "were you working the night Kendal Mardell was shot to death in here?"

"Yes, yes, I was. So was Wayne, the owner. Whoever shot the coach knew we would be too busy to pay attention to anything out of the ordinary.

"A dart tournament took up most of the room from where we're standing to the front door. It's a traveling tourney, six bars in all. It was our Thursday night to host. There wouldn't have been a fourth of the folks here if it weren't dart night."

"What can you tell me about the coach?" I asked.

"Sweet guy, married, three kids, wife of, I think I heard twenty something years. Loved by the players and the parents."

"Apparently someone didn't like him. Can you tell me anything about that night?" Amy asked.

"Not much to tell. Coach sat on a stool facing the dining area. He was in the dart tourney. The noise was so loud my eardrums pounded like a dozen kettle drums all played at the same time. Wayne was in the walk-in cooler out back. He saw a white limo drive up. Said he could hardly wait to see who had rented it.

"Next thing I knew one of our regulars let out a shout, *'Something's wrong with coach!'*. It wasn't until a few minutes later we realized he'd been shot and wasn't breathing. Two or three of the guys ran to the parking lot, but all they saw was the limo driving away.

"One of the women said she noticed the shooter when she came in. Said she looked so out of place, dressed to the nines. Only two things stood out about her. She wore a huge ring on her left ring finger, and she had a tattoo on her wrist; a tiny two-toned heart."

"Who saw the tattoo?" I asked.

"Johnny Wade," she said. "He and I went to high school together. He's not a drinker. He bumped into her. He was on his way in and she was on the way out. He didn't try to stop her because he didn't know anything had happened inside.

"I heard him tell the police that even though she was small, she didn't move when he ran into her. He described her as like *he hit a brick wall*."

"We'll take a glass of wine if you have Moscato. I'm not ready to face the traffic to get back to the city."

Tiffany poured two glasses and set them on the bar. "On the house," she said.

I took out a twenty and put it next to the wine. "Thanks, but it's against the rules. Do you care where we sit?"

She grinned again. "No, pick your spot. Are you sure you are worried about the rules. I thought cops couldn't drink on the job."

I laughed. "We are only filling in because of the pandemic. It isn't like they can fire us." I gave her my biggest smile.

Amy asked, "how often does Johnny Wade come in?"

"He's here now." She cocked her head toward a four top in the corner with three men eating lunch. "He's the guy with his back to you."

"Thanks," Amy said and looked at me. "I'm going to invite him over for a chat. I'd sure like to know more about the tattoo. I think what he said about running into her and how strong she was is very interesting. Makes me wonder if we are looking for a man and don't know it?"

Johnny had a burger, onion rings and a Coke in front of him. Amy whispered something to him and he glanced back toward me and smiled. I nodded at him and smiled back.

"Tiffany didn't say he was gorgeous when she told

us about him," Amy chuckled as she sat back down at our table.

"Maybe she saw the wedding rings on our fingers and didn't think it was worth mentioning," I said.

Amy laughed. "I don't want to take him home, but I will sure enjoy looking at him for the next few minutes. He'll be over in a few. Tiffany said he and the guys he's with are here on a lunch break. They work at the Amazon warehouse."

We drank our wine and looked closer at our surroundings. The killer would only have had to walk two or three steps into the bar, shoot, drop the gun and walk out. Now that Tiffany had filled in some details, I could see why no one had heard the shots. I estimated forty men and women in the establishment. Most were having lunch. One young couple played pool, and I noticed most everyone had a soft drink rather than a beer. The old saying, *it's five o'clock somewhere* came to mind.

Within ten minutes, Johnny Wade came over to our table. Amy didn't lie. His dark wavy hair curled around his ears and on the back of his neck, but he didn't look as if he really needed a haircut. He had mesmerizing Zac Efron eyes. I gauged him as about six-feet-four and a bodybuilder.

"May I sit?" he asked

I didn't realize until then I'd been staring at him. Amy kicked me under the table in an *I told you so.* gesture. "Sure," I said, "we'd like to clear a couple of things up from your interview with the police the night Kendal Mardell was shot."

"Sure," he said, showing more of his snow white, even teeth.

Amy laid a folder, she'd been holding under her arm, on the table and opened it. The sticker on the front read, *Kendall Mardell Homicide.* "It says here you were coming into the bar as the killer was leaving. Tell us what you remember."

Johnny held his empty soda glass toward Tiffany. "Can you make me a Coke to go?" He asked. He turned his attention back to Amy, he came straight out of a Dale Carnegie, *How to Win Friends and Influence People* book. "Not only did we meet at the door but she nearly shoved me out of the way so she could leave. I thought she was about to fall so I grabbed her arm. She shoved me back with so much force I couldn't believe it."

"What about the tattoo you saw on her left wrist?"

"It would have been hard to miss. It was a tiny heart, the thing that made it stand out was the colors; red on top, an odd pink on the bottom and the broken heart line separating the two pieces. I swear, if I hadn't seen her fine features, I would have thought she was a man.

"I don't think the tattoo was real. The edges were blurry. It actually looked like someone drew it on with a magic marker."

I leaned toward him. "You saw her? I don't see anything about that in the report. Did you tell the police what you saw?"

"I did, but the cop sort of brushed me off, like she didn't want the information."

"Do you remember her name?"

"Yes, it's a name you couldn't forget once you heard or saw it; Clara Clark."

"One more thing," Amy said, "think you can describe her to a police sketch artist?"

"I know this will sound crazy, but I didn't actually see her face. I saw just enough to know she was a small woman."

"That makes no sense," I said.

He looked me in the eye. "Have you ever looked at your watch and when somebody asked you what time it is two minutes later, you can't tell them without looking at your watch again?

"It's because we want to know what time it is in correlation to lunch time, dinner time or when our favorite TV show is on. Stuff like that. It's what happened to me. I looked at her long enough to know she was a woman, but if you wanted me to describe her, I would have to see her again.

"I saw her for an instant. When I bumped into her, I thought she was a man. Her looks told me she was female. It's truly all I saw. My mind was focused on the noise inside, the gun I nearly tripped over on my way inside and people yelling for someone to call 911.

"The car is another matter. It was an old Cadillac stretch limo with the tag, ENUFSENUF and it was issued by the State of Confusion. I stopped to look at it. The windows were tinted so dark I couldn't see a thing. I knocked on the driver's window to see if he'd let me take a look, but I got no response."

"Thanks for your help," we said in unison.

He turned to leave. "I told the police lady about the sticker on the back window, but she didn't make a note of it."

"Tell me about it," Amy said.

"ENUFSENUF, Coalition for The Right to Live."

Amy wrote down what he said and turned it toward him. "That is what is said but it was on four lines:

"ENUFSENUF Coalition for Right to Live."

He looked at how Amy adjusted the words. "That's it. The top part of the sticker was red and had the first two lines in white lettering. The bottom of the sticker was white with red lettering and had the last two lines in red.

"It wasn't very big, maybe three inches wide and two inches high. Had I not stopped to study the car, I wouldn't have seen it."

He looked at his watch. "I need to go. My lunch hour is nearly over."

"One last thing," I said. "Is the only person you gave this information to, this Clara Clark?"

"Yes."

He started toward the door. "Did she have the same uniform as everyone else?"

He stopped for a minute. "I think so. There was a lot going on."

"Thanks again," I said.

CHAPTER 11

Once we were in the car, I asked Amy what time it was.

She said, "If we leave now, go down Earth City Expressway to the Maryland Height's Parkway to 270 and take it to Ladue Road, we can beat the traffic to University City."

"After our discussion with Johnny Wade, I'll never look at the time the same way again," I said, "but he's right."

"Are you thinking the same thing I am?" She asked.

"That we should go back to the office and investigate Officer Clark?"

"Yes. Something else I noticed. The young man at the restaurant said the tattoo was on her right arm and there was a watch band on the left. Johnny Wade said the tattoo was on the left hand and he didn't mention a watch band."

"True, it makes me think the tattoo is a distractor. I don't know what to think of the watch yet."

"I agree. I haven't heard from the guys all day, have

you?"

"There's a text here from Nathan. *Don't go home, don't cook. I'm bringing the dogs and beer. Ryan is picking up steaks and the rest of the fixings to have a great BBQ. Unless you have a better idea, I'll see you there. Had a great day, hope you did."* She stopped reading and her face turned scarlet. "The rest of the message is for me," she said.

Chili and Axel were ecstatic to see us. Chili got so excited she peed on me. It had to be in joy because once Axel had been at the house long enough to learn to guard her when Ryan and I weren't around, we put in a doggy door. They could come and go out to the yard and back any time they wanted. Axel never let Chili stay in the house when he was out or let her be outside without him.

Making Axel a member of the family was one of the best decisions we ever made.

Off the kitchen we had a bedroom and bathroom. Both of the rooms were bigger than what Ryan and I had upstairs in the master suite.

Amy got bitten by a deadly snake once and she and Nathan lived in those rooms for several weeks. They dubbed it the *Maid's Quarters*. The walls were a daisy yellow, the carpet a dark brown and the quilt and furnishings were a combination of the two. I found it relaxing. On the rare occasion I ended up at home alone, I took a nap in there.

The bathroom had a huge shower and a walk-in tub.

Since the four of us were so close, they kept extra clothes and necessities in the room. Amy headed to take a shower and change into something more comfortable. I went upstairs to do the same.

Both dogs went up with me and lounged on the bed until I finished up and headed back down. I heard the garage door open and, in a minute, the door to the kitchen. Sally and Digger ran in. Behind them were Ryan and Nathan, each with bags full of food.

Amy came out of the Maid's Quarters dressed in torn jeans, a Chicago White Sox tee that had seen better days and no shoes.

I'd changed into jeans, so old the knees were about gone, and a faded maroon Hollister tee shirt. I had slipped on Nike sandals.

Once the guys put the bags down, they greeted us properly; as properly as one can in public. The dogs had a ten minute free-for-all. I finally commanded them to go outside.

Amy walked over to the counter. "What's in the bags?"

"Surprises," Ryan said, "when Kate messaged me, she said you had some research you were excited about. You ladies go ahead with your work and Nathan and I will call when dinner's ready."

"Sounds good," Amy said, and we headed toward the front of the house to the office.

After months of people trying to kill us, having to wait for information from the homicide department downtown and the FBI, Ryan tore out the wall between to of the front rooms and built an office.

We had state of the art equipment. If we couldn't find the facts we needed and Jacob, Ryan's tech guy couldn't find it on the dark web, we knew it couldn't be found.

Clara Clark, Amy wrote on our dry erase board. "Are you real?"

I checked the statewide police employee database. Since we could practically throw a stone to Illinois, I checked there also. No one by the name of Clara and no one with the last name Clark came up in the list.

Amy had the same luck with the FBI.

She tried a national list of non-profit coalitions while I searched fringe groups. A big fat nothing—there was no coalition and no Clara Clark. A loud commotion started in the hall outside the office door. "I'd say dinner is ready, Amy."

We shut down the computers and headed toward the kitchen.

I could smell the meat on the barbeque grill as soon as we opened the door. Ryan liked to use charcoal. Two glasses of white wine sat on the table along with a Caesar salad in four separate bowls, one by each plate, and a bigger bowl sitting in a large aluminum bowl of ice chips. Baked potatoes were dressed with butter, sour cream, shredded cheddar cheese and chives.

Amy sat down in a chair opposite me, picked up her wine glass and looked my way. Once I picked mine up, she said, "A toast to the world's two greatest husbands."

"What did we do to deserve this?" I asked, but they only smiled and looked at one another. "Okay, what's up?"

"First of all," Ryan said, "we would have done this anyway." He moved his arm to encompass all the food and the grill. "But I was invited to Jupiter, Florida for a few days to take a look at the security down there. I thought Nathan might want to go along."

Amy and I both laughed. We knew they were telling the truth. The men liked each other, both liked to cook and have a beer or two and both were huge Cardinal fans. "When are you leaving?" Amy asked.

"We thought maybe Monday. With the dogs, I think you are both safe, either at each of our houses or here if Amy feels better about it."

I looked at Amy. "It's up to you. I love having you here, and all four dogs get along famously."

"Let me think about it," she said. "Nathan, you know I love you but sometimes to have one's house to one's self is like a vacation."

"Amen," I said.

We finished dinner and moved away from the table to a little area Ryan and I had set up with a firepit, a love seat, two comfy chairs and small tables where needed. I was on my third glass of wine and the guys their third beer when all four dogs began to bark and run around the yard. They all chased an object in the air they couldn't reach, and it frustrated them. The color told us it wasn't a toy and whoever guided it knew what they were doing.

Ryan ran to the middle of the dogs and jumped to try to reach the object, which we all knew by now was a drone. Nathan, who stood a good four inches taller than Ryan, couldn't touch it either. It became a moot point when the drone dropped a manilla envelope and soared off.

"Don't anyone touch that. We want to dust it for fingerprints," I said.

Without hesitation I ran back to the office and got a kit. Not a fingerprint nor a smudge could be found. "I guess we should see what's inside. I have a bad feeling about it," I said.

Amy added, "it gives off a negative vibe."

We might not have known what it contained, but we certainly could guess who it came from.

CHAPTER 12

Amy and I quickly cleaned the dishes off the table and took the leftover food into the kitchen. We wanted to sit so we could all observe when Ryan sliced the flat envelope open with his pocket knife.

Four small pictures fell out, along with a letter and a drawing. The pictures were of Victor Mann, Dennis Small and Kendall Mardell.

We couldn't identify the man in the fourth picture. He wore a suit and tie and sat in what looked like a comfy office chair. His face had been blacked out. Had it been with a magic marker or white out, we might have been able to reverse the damage and bring his features back. Whoever sent the photo scratched out the face with something sharp. To try to restore it would have been a lost cause.

The first three pictures were labeled on the back with their names. The names were in newspaper print. The metro area in which we lived had at least twenty small, medium and large newspapers. Picking out which one the print came from presented another dead end.

The word NEXT in capital letters with a black magic marker was pasted on the last photo.

The letter said; *Stop this nonsense. We would hate to add any of you to our list because we know you haven't done anything.*

Once we rid the area of the people on our list, we will be done. Some of them have figured it out and gone into hiding. For these men, and a few more, their time has come. Stay out of the way and stay safe. YOU HAVE BEEN WARNED.

The last pieces of paper showed a close up of wrists. The first had a tattoo of a broken heart. The signature said *People Who Have Had Enuf. We have had enough of these people living happy lives while we waste away in despair and unhappiness.*

Ryan looked at each one of us in turn. "Knowing you ladies the way I do. I know you aren't going to back down. I don't think it's a good time to go on a trip, you agree, Nathan?"

"I certainly do."

Amy smiled at her husband. "Honey, I was a patrolman on the streets of Chicago for ten years. I'm not afraid of a vigilante with an agenda to kill men she, or they, consider evil."

"And you?" Ryan asked me. "Do you feel the same?"

"You know I do. Go on your trip, have fun."

They both said *no* at the same time.

The rest of the evening, we tried to come up with reasons someone would want to kill these men. From the note, I had to think they were all murdered for the same reason. We came up with adultery, blackmail, extortion, child molestation, fraud, embezzlement, money laundering, tax evasion, forgery, drugs, human trafficking and racism.

I said, "I feel like we are reaching. What are the chances all four men were selling drugs, child molesters, or all committed adultery and ticked off these people enough to want them dead?"

"Slim to none," Amy said. "We need to check their ages, schools they attended, churches, clubs and organizations they belonged to and check into their finances. Maybe they are paying someone off for a bad deed they were involved in. What is going to make this easier is that if one of them doesn't fit in; they are all disqualified."

"They could all be professional hits," Ryan added. "If so, I don't know if we can catch them. Have you thought about blowing up the pictures of the wrists? I think the tattoos are fake, they are not even in the same spot on the wrists. If they were a real clue, they wouldn't highlight them in a picture."

CHAPTER 13

When Amy and Nathan left to go home at about eleven, we still hadn't talked our husbands into going on their trip to the Cardinal's Spring Training.

Amy and I agreed to meet back at the office the next morning. They had no sooner backed Nathan's truck out of the driveway when the police scanner radio Roger Simon had given me began to squeal.

If mine made noise, then so did the one Amy had been given.

Sure enough, within a few minutes, Amy and Nathan were back in the house. I pressed the button to hear dispatch. On the other end a voice said: *Homicide at 2036 Benton Road, the Benjamin Highland home. Officers on the scene. Please respond.*

"10-4," I said into the speaker and ran upstairs to grab a jacket, my badge and my Glock.

I carried a 9mm Glock 42; Amy preferred a Ruger.

Nathan and Ryan, who were registered to carry concealed firearms, each had a Walther.

We were on the road in nothing flat. I drove my Land Rover because Roger had had it equipped with the police radio I asked for, scanner, siren and lights. Benton Road, in the Ladue area, supported houses of around seven hundred thousand dollars to a few million.

I guessed the one we pulled up to at about two and a half million dollars. It was colonial style with four white pillars and a six-car attached garage. The home had professional landscaping. The outside lights were on. I could see the last blooms of what had been a beautiful flower garden.

Another four car garage sat at an angle off to the right of the house. The property, from what I could see, looked to be about three acres. Pieces of a car were everywhere. There were so many parts scattered within a 250-foot radius, it would be impossible, without the lab, to tell what model and make of car it used to be.

We would have run over debris had we pulled into the driveway. I parked the Rover down the street, out of the way of the dozens of official cars, two ambulances, four fire trucks, six cruisers with lights twirling and a van with the word 'Coroner' painted on the side. Ryan parked his truck behind me. We all got out of the cars and walked up to the scene together.

A closer look showed the blast to be powerful enough to have taken off the entire attached garage and part of what I assumed to be the kitchen of the big stucco mansion.

We passed a St. Louis County Sheriff's car at the entrance to the subdivision and a Highway Patrol cruiser blocking the egress to the street. Another Ladue police car with a patrol officer standing beside it sat at the entrance to the driveway. At the entrance and exit of the street, were two more patrol cars. Highway Patrol cruisers sat at the entrance to the subdivision. I had to show ID to get us closer to the scene.

We couldn't tell if this bombing had anything to do with Enuf is Enuf. The Bomb Squad sat halfway down the driveway. Men clad in white Explosive Ordnance Disposal suits (EOD) dug through the debris. Mike Anderson, the chief, walked toward us. "I'm not sure what the goal was here, but someone blew up Benjamin Highland, and let his wife go into the house before they detonated.

"She's pretty torn up. All we have so far is they went to a play at the local high school. Their grandson had a part. Afterwards they went to Ted Drew's for an ice cream, and strolled through a car show at the Steak 'n Shake up the street from there. When they arrived home, her husband let her out of the car before he pulled into the driveway because she wanted to look at something in the side garden. She said she had only just gone into the house when it shook and something exploded.

"My guess is it was set off with a cell phone or, if the killer was close enough, they could have used a switch."

"Thanks, Mike. Let us know if you find anything to help us. We'll go inside and speak to Mrs. Highland," I said.

"Emma, Emma Highland. She is the principle at one of the Christian schools. Not sure which one," Mike said.

"And him?" Amy asked.

"I'm surprised you don't know. He owns three

restaurants on the Hill, two downtown by the stadium and has chefs at three or four of the best hotels around."

"So our suspect pool is likely thousands," I said.

I called to Ryan, "Do you know Benjamin Highland?"

He looked around the rubble. "Is that who this is? Yes, of course I know him. One of the restaurants he owns is The Mazy."

"The seafood restaurant downtown?"

"One in the same. I wonder how he ended up in this mystery?"

"Right now I don't know how anyone did. Could you and Nathan go to the neighbors for about a mile each way and see if they caught anything on camera or saw anything unusual?"

"What if they ask us for a badge?"

"Don't give them a chance. Say I'm with the investigation of the bombing at the Highland home. Then ask your questions. I doubt anyone is asleep or didn't hear the explosion. They have no idea what happened, and I bet they are all on edge. Tell them if we determine they are in any danger, someone will be back.

"Your goal is to get information, not to give it. The best answer to give if they push you is, no one has been identified. I'm sure you will be some of the first to find out what happened.

"You're good at this, aren't you. We are on our way." Ryan leaned over and pecked me on the cheek. "This is the first time I've been at a real crime scene with the big boss. I'm impressed."

I playfully pushed him away. Amy and I walked to the front door, which stood wide open.

CHAPTER 14

Emma Highland stood at the far end of a massive room. In her hands she held a Kleenex. She held it in both hands as one would a blanket. I finally knew what the saying, *wringing her hands*, really meant. Her green eyes were red and swollen from crying.

I stood barely five feet one and Mrs. Highland's height ranged somewhere between there and Amy's five feet ten. "Sit down," she said when we entered the room. She didn't bother to ask who we were so I began to introduce myself. "I'm Kate..." She stopped me before I got my last name out. "Miss Nash, or is it Mrs. Mead? Is there anyone within a hundred mile radius who doesn't know who you are? The question is, why are you here?" She said it as though I was quite a bother.

My face grew hot. I did my best not to change my facial expression. "At the request of the St. Louis authorities, my partner Amy Perkin and I are joining the homicide division of the police department until they have enough people back to work due to Covid.

"I worked in homicide for ten years and Miss Perkin has been in law enforcement for more than fifteen years. Your investigation is in good hands."

"So, can you tell me who killed my husband and why?"

"Not in the first ten minutes," Amy said. She did less to hide her distaste than I did. "Let's have a seat and you can tell us about your day. It might help."

While Amy talked, I'd been watching Mrs. Highland. She reeked of money and finishing school. I speculated, Brown, Mount Holyoke or Spelman. She had a two hundred dollar hairdo and her makeup had been specially blended to her skin tone.

Diamonds sparkled on every finger. None were as big as the solitaire around her neck on a silver chain. One didn't have to guess, she thought she deserved a position of power and elevation and she intended to have it. Who was I to say she didn't deserve it?

Emma must have pushed a button, because a pretty young maid in full uniform came in and stood by the door. "Ellen, could you bring us," she looked from Amy to me, "do you prefer coffee or tea, or perhaps iced tea?"

"Nothing for me," I said.

She ignored me and said to the maid, "We'll take three iced teas with lemon, please."

"Mrs. Highland, the girl said, "there are men boarding up the kitchen. Police are everywhere. The best I can do for you and your guests is fetch some bottled water."

I can't describe the look on Mrs. Highland's face. It didn't seem like the face of someone who only minutes ago lost a husband. She couldn't hide her disappointment in being disappointed.

The maid stood quietly. When the lady of the house didn't say anything, she nodded her head and backed out of the room.

After what seemed an hour but probably only took a minute or two, we sat down. I started. "Mrs. Highland, we understand you had an evening out. Did anything out of the ordinary happen?"

"I didn't think so at first," she said, "but Ben mentioned a big white car following us. He was quite taken with it. I thought it was probably from a car show we walked through earlier in the evening. He loves...," she dropped her head into her hands. Amy and I looked at one another. I wanted to say something yet I wanted to give her time to get control. Before I opened my mouth to speak, the maid arrived with three bottles of water, three stemmed water glasses and a small bowl of lemon slices on a tray. "Is there anything else, Mrs.?"

Mrs. Highland didn't answer. She dismissed the girl with a wave of her hand.

I wondered if Amy had the same thoughts I did. Here we sat, in a formal living room with the woman's husband blown into at least a thousand pieces not fifty feet from us, but we were having ice water as if nothing was amiss.

"I didn't know I was so parched. I've never had my husband murdered before," she said.

"Can we go back to the white car?" I asked. "Can you tell me anything about it?"

"No, but Ben said it was an older Cadillac. A limousine, I think. We don't use a car service," she continued. "Ben loves to drive."

"How many times did you see the car?" Amy asked.

"Well, it was at the play, I guess, because it followed us to the restaurant. I didn't see it in the parking lot of the school or the restaurant. When we finished eating, the valet gave us our car and when we pulled out of the lot, the car pulled out behind us."

I asked, "Didn't you find it odd?"

"We did at first, we believed it was following us but Ben laughed and said, no one is going to tail you in an old model stretch limo, especially a white one. I doubt there are many in service around. It's just a coincidence."

"Did it follow you home?" Amy asked.

"Yes, it did, but when we pulled into the driveway, it drove on past."

"What happened when you got out of the car? Why didn't you go into the garage with your husband? Do you always go in the front?"

"No, not usually. There was an item on the sidewalk. We couldn't see what it was, but I said I would look so he could go on inside and let the dog out."

"What did you find on the sidewalk?"

"I believe it was the control that set off the bomb that killed my Benjamin." I could see she tried to be stoic, but her feelings finally worked their way through her perceived demeanor. She cried so hard it was all I could do to keep from crying myself. When I looked toward Amy, her eyes were filled with tears about to spill over and down her cheeks. I had to get control of the grieving lady. "Do you have the device?"

"No, I gave it to the first officer on the scene. She was here within a minute. She said she was down the street because someone saw a strange person in their yard. She didn't find anything out of the ordinary and when she heard the explosion, she came here."

"Do you have her name?"

"Yes, she gave me her card. I slipped it in my pocket." She took it out and handed it to Amy.

"Clara Clark. What did she look like?"

Mrs. Highland looked alarmed. "Don't you know her?"

Amy smiled. "We are filling in. There are thousands of officers we've never met. Can you tell us what she looked like, maybe we can find her outside?"

"She was about five feet six, had long brown hair. As a matter of fact, she looked more like a model than a police officer. And you won't find her outside. She took the button thing from me, handed me her card, and about then she received a call and had to leave."

I asked, "Does your husband have any enemies that you know of?"

"Oh, probably. We have six restaurants and dozens of hotels we take care of room service for. It is impossible to keep everyone happy. For the most part he's well-liked."

I stood, "We won't bother you any more tonight, Mrs. Highland. Do you want us to call someone for you? You might not want to stay here. There is no way to close the garage off. The fire department called a service they use to board up buildings after a fire. We know someone closed up the kitchen but the garage is a crime scene."

"I called my daughter. She is coming after me. Ellen is packing my things now."

"Do you have a phone number where we can reach you?"

She gave it to us and we got up to leave. "Did you see the car Officer Clark left in?"

"No, I came inside and she walked down the driveway. If her car was parked on the street, I wouldn't be able to see it from the house."

CHAPTER 15

A my and I had a ritual. Every morning she dropped by a coffee shop on the University City Loop and picked up two tall lattes. I kept blueberry bagels and cream cheese at the house. Sometimes she brought the dogs and sometimes not. After the drone, I wanted Axel close to me.

Amy left Digger and Sally home to guard their house.

I liked the days we met at the coffee shop and ate and drank there. I don't know what the magic was, but the lattes always tasted better, the bagels were crispier and the cream cheese smoother at our local Starbucks. People in the case we were working on were dropping like soldiers in a war zone. It seemed safer to eat at the office.

"By the way," I said when I sat down at the kitchen table, "there aren't many white Cadillac Limos in the five surrounding states. Black cars seem to be much more popular.

"I believe whoever is driving the car bought it from

a person who modified two cars into a limo."

Amy said, "I've been thinking about the car, too. Are they trying to get caught? Every cop in the area has the description and the plate. I don't know how they drove around all night without anyone spotting them."

I finished my latte and filled a paper cup with plain coffee left from what Ryan made before he left. Amy held hers up for me to do the same. "Why did they bomb the last victim? Until we talked to Emma Highland, I thought it was to take the noticeable car out of the equation. I'm obviously wrong."

Amy picked up Chili who happened to be walking by. "I couldn't get to sleep last night trying to figure out what they did with the car. There are so many cameras, cell phones and nosey people, I'd think at least one person had to see it. I believe 90 % of the population now has a doorbell camera.

I petted Axel's head. He wanted equal attention. "I believe it is parked in a garage somewhere covered up, or maybe they drive it into a truck and then drive the truck to a safe location."

"Kate, I think you are right about the truck. Let's look at the film from cameras around the murder scenes and see if we can spot the same truck within a block or two of them."

I could feel the excitement in the room. Finally, an action we could move forward on.

We each took crime scene photos and videos and began to look for a truck large enough to drive a limo into. I looked it up and the average stretch limo spans 30 feet.

Security tapes from five cameras should have picked up something. I watched the one from the church first.

It showed a person come in the front door. The pew camera took over. Looked like she leaned over and said a few words to the man sitting in the last row. These films had no sound. I watched the flash of the gun, one, two, three, four.

No one turned around. She shot him as the priest pronounced the couple at the front of the church, man and wife, and the large crowd went wild. I doubt you could've heard yourself think at that moment.

After watching all five videos, we thought we'd found what we believed to be the same truck within a mile of each crime scene.

On the sides were pictures of furniture. A couch, chair, and a hammock with a pretty blond laying in it. The words, Morgenstern Delivery Service, Cottleville, Missouri in big red letters was prominent on the side facing toward the cameras.

Cottleville had a population of around five thousand people and sat in St. Charles County. I called Roger. "Any progress on the murders?" He asked before I had a chance to tell him why I called.

"A little," I said. "We think we know how they are hiding the limo. They pull it into an independent furniture truck out of Cottleville. See if you can get the St. Charles County authorities to check around and see if they can find it. Painted on the sides are the words Morgenstern Delivery Service, Cottleville, Missouri. It looks new, no noticeable dents or missing paint. You can't miss it. The name is painted in red and takes up the entire side of the truck from front to back. Also there are pictures of furniture. Not something you would soon forget."

"Are we sure the bombing was done by the same

people?"

"We think so because the limo was seen several times during the evening. I have no idea why no police recognize it; we have a description everywhere except on the sides of buildings. It followed the Highlands all evening. It even sat in parking lots, and yet, nothing."

Once I explained about the furniture truck, Roger said he would get the authorities right on the job of finding it.

"One more thing, Roger, have you ever heard of a cop, about five feet six, long brown hair, the looks of a model, who goes by the name, Clara Clark?"

"No. And that's a name I wouldn't forget," he said.

Amy and I put the dogs in my Range Rover and drove to Cottleville. They loved to go for a ride. "Want to go by the house and pick up Digger and Sally?"

She said, "They are at camp today. Nathan thinks it is good for them to go once a week and become socialized. Sally scares people to death just because she's a Rot. We walk them most nights and even the people we see every evening shy away from her. She's such a sweet dog."

"If I didn't know her, I'd shy away," I said.

We scoured the Walmart parking lot, front and back, Target, the college and the golf course. We didn't see any furniture stores or factories. Except for the two big box stores, the town businesses were mostly restaurants.

Amy stayed in the car while I paid a visit to the local police department. It looked the same as most departments I'd been in, but much smaller.

A uniformed officer walked past me and I said, "Excuse me, I'm with St. Louis Homicide." As I spoke,

I flashed my badge.

"Are you the reason the entire force," he smiled, "all five of them are out looking for a delivery truck?"

"Yes, I guess I am. Has anyone seen it?"

He took off his hat, twirled it slowly in his hands by the band and said, "No Miss, there is no truck like that around here. We all live in town, and one of us would have seen it somewhere."

"So did you actually go look for it, or did you just decide from what you already know, it isn't here?"

He put his hat back on and pushed it back off of his forehead. "No, Detective, we looked. We checked all of the barns and buildings large enough to hold a truck like that. There was nothing. Sorry we couldn't be of more help. Your Captain told us it was related to the murders all over the area. We'd like to put an end to that."

"Dennis Small was a good friend of the mayor," the cop said.

"Sorry to hear that. Thanks for your help."

I felt his eyes on me as I walked to the door and opened it to leave.

CHAPTER 16

W e hadn't made it back to the office before Roger called. "We found your Cadillac Limo. It is in the Mississippi River near the Ameristar Casino. They picked a terrible place if they wanted to keep it quiet. Hundreds, if not thousands, of people visit the casino every day."

"Who saw it go in the water?" I asked.

"Last I heard, about a hundred and twenty people were on a dinner cruise, when it happened, a couple dozen were standing above deck at the railing and saw the car go in the water. No one saw anyone go in or come out of the water. A patrolman by the name of Simon Peters is holding them on the boat until you get there."

"Okay, we are on our way," I said.

Even though we were close to the casino we went to the house and dropped off the dogs. The high temperatures made it impossible to leave them in the car.

The cruise ship, called *The Admiral*, had docked

about two hundred yards down from a riverboat casino. There were folks standing at the deck railing when the car went into the water. Officer Peters had detained everyone on the boat and had them all sitting at tables in the dining room. Along with them, the boat's crew and captain tried to keep them comfortable with iced tea and coffee.

Amy spoke first. "I'm Detective Amy Perkin, St. Louis Homicide, and this is my partner Detective Kate Nash."

A low pitched murmur sounded across the room. I hated moments like these. People knew who I was for all the wrong reasons. Why couldn't they know me as a great philanthropist instead of a woman who got arrested in front of her own home and brought up on murder charges because her doppelganger was thought to be a felon?

It didn't help I married one of the richest men in the area, perhaps in the country, or that a young woman had died on our front stoop. It had been a little too exciting of a year.

I took a deep breath and pushed my anger and embarrassment to the back of my mind so we could get on with our investigation.

"I'll interview some of you at the table over here." I pointed to a table in the corner of the room. "Detective Perkin will interview the other half of you over there." Again I pointed to a table. If you were not in a position to see the car go into the river, you may leave. Give your name, address and phone number to Officer Peters before you go."

I nodded to a young couple who looked to be about twenty. "We can start with you."

They walked toward me as if they were going to the gallows. "Have a seat," I said, as I took a small notebook out of my back pocket.

The couple sat close together; their fingers intertwined. The color drained out of the girl's face while his, on the other hand, turned bright red. "You are not in any trouble," I began. "I'd like for you to tell me what you saw this evening pertaining to the white limo going into the water. Let's start with your names."

The young man mumbled something, and I laid my hand on the table with a little more force than necessary. "Listen, this isn't an inquisition. You happened to see a car, which we believe has been used as the getaway car in several murders, go into the water. Tell me what you saw and you can get out of here."

The young man straightened up. The girl leaned harder on him. "Ellie, this is Ellie Martin, she and I, I'm Tom Daily. We were standing on the top deck watching the skyline when a white car, a limousine, drove into the water and sank."

"Tom," I said, "you said drove into the water. Did you see anyone in or around the car?"

"No. As soon as I saw the car was going to sink, I looked down, took my phone out and dialed 911."

I looked toward the girl. "What about you?"

"I closed my eyes. I really didn't see." Tears began to fill her eyes and run down her cheeks.

"Here is what I want you to do. Go over to the policeman standing in front of the door. Give him your name and address and then you can go."

They bolted like a couple of cats with tin cans tied to their tails.

It took until way after midnight to talk to everyone.

On the way home, Amy and I compared notes. It actually turned out to be simple. Someone let the car roll from the top of the levee near the arch, a no parking or driving zone. It gained speed and might have been going as fast as twenty when it hit the water. A busy sidewalk ran along the edge of the levee. Thank goodness no one got hurt as the car came down the hill to the river.

All the windows were down on the car so it sank quickly. No people were seen in or around the car. Our killers knew human nature. They knew no one would be watching anything around the area other than the huge old white limo as it splashed into the water and sunk head first.

We left long before the wrecker pulled the car from the Mississippi River. We headed for the police forensic garage. Amy and I both knew there would be nothing to find inside the car.

CHAPTER 17

We didn't go by the house to pick up Amy's car. She could ride over in the morning with Nathan. Ryan stood inside the kitchen door when I opened it. "I can't say as I like these late hours. Is this the way it was when you were a homicide detective?"

I walked over to kiss him. "Pretty much," I said, "you have to stay with a murder or murders every minute or the killers get ahead of you. Look at it this way, I won't be doing this again. Amy and I, both together and separately told Roger, this is our one and only case."

He took me in his arms and rested his chin on the top of my head. "Hungry?"

"Starved."

"Good, I called Aldo's and had them send over a chicken Caesar salad and an order of garlic bread. I have a bottle of Rose' chilling in the cooler."

"It's so nice to be the wife of someone who owns restaurants," I said.

He kissed the top of my head again before he moved to the island in the kitchen. I stayed on the dining room side as he walked around to the prep and cook area. "I ordered a ham and Swiss on rye. If it sounds good to you, I'll share it."

"The garlic bread sounds better than anything. Hope it has cheese."

"You know it will have cheese. I know what you like." He said it with an inflection which alerted me he wasn't talking about food.

Ryan must have ordered the food the minute I messaged how long it would take me to drive home. Because the food arrived only minutes after we said hello.

We both sat at the bar. He stayed on his side and me on mine. It took all my concentration not to gobble down the food.

"Tell me about your evening," he said. "All we got from the news was that a white limo went into the water near the casino and there were no bodies in or around the accident. A source close to the investigation said it was believed the car was the get-away car in the recent murders in the area."

"It wasn't an accident. Someone drove the car up to the levy and pointed it toward the water. It was going at a pretty good clip when it hit. It sank immediately."

"Any idea why?" He asked.

"I have a theory. The man they blew up in his garage tonight was their last victim. The only two clues we had were the car and the truck. We believe they sunk the car to hide it in plain sight.

"The car is now gone and we haven't found the truck. They are now going to go back to whatever they did before they were vigilantes and we will never catch them."

"So you and Amy are giving up? What does Roger say about that?"

I held up my glass for him to fill it again. "You know me better than that. I won't give up until the killers are on death row. Just frustrated. Where are the dogs?"

He laughed as he said, "they went to bed. Last time I went upstairs, they were both snoring. Great watch dogs, huh?"

Ryan had greeted me at the door in a pair of lounge pants and a tee shirt. When we went upstairs, he went into the bathroom and brushed his teeth. Back in the bedroom, he pulled the covers down. While I brushed my teeth and washed my face, I could tell he listened to the messages on his phone.

I crawled in next to him in time to take the phone as it slipped from his hand. Sleep caught him before I could kiss him goodnight. He turned on his side and I turned on mine. I snuggled close to his chest, he instinctively put his arms around me and I went to sleep.

Chili woke me up with a cold tongue in my ear. "Hi there, squirt. Where are Axel and Ryan?"

I always talked to the dogs as though they would answer me.

Voices drifted up from downstairs and when I glanced at the clock, I was shocked I'd slept until eight-thirty. I needed to stop over-sleeping. I didn't think it would happen until the case ended. Every aspect of it seemed to happen at night.

After a quick shower I lassoed my thick red, unruly

hair into a low ponytail.

My house keeping skills were nil. There were more clothes on the floor of my closet than hanging up. Ryan and I had his and hers closets, thank goodness. I picked a light blue blouse still in the plastic sleeve from the cleaners, a pair of navy jeans, my trademark spike heels in navy blue, and a navy blazer with white piping around the collar, cuffs and button holes as well as white buttons.

I carried Chili down the stairs in one arm and my jacket in the other. No use putting it on since my Glock and holster were stowed on top of the refrigerator.

"Hello, sleepyhead," Amy said. "I decided to give you fifteen more minutes and then I was going to set off the alarm."

"I wonder why Ryan didn't wake me. I suppose he is gone already?"

"Yes, but he left a note. I didn't turn it over for fear it would burn my eyes."

I picked it up and smiled. "It's rated PG," I said. "He has a dinner with the owner of a small business in Nixa. I have seen little of him since we agreed to take this case."

"Same here," she said. "We stayed up last night and had pizza and wine, just to spend a little time together. I got the same message as you except Nathan's dinner meeting is in O'Fallon, Illinois."

"I think our killers have accomplished their goal. I'll be surprised if we have to go out. Should we go get your dogs so they don't have to be alone all day?"

"Nathan is going to drop them off later. Both of them had shots due and Sally is gaining weight. We want to make sure she is only over eating and nothing else is wrong."

"What do you want to do first?" I asked.

"How about a latte and bagel. I didn't eat yet, I waited for you."

"Aren't you sweet?"

She grinned at me. Her skin looked as though it had never seen the sun. I knew she didn't wear makeup; she didn't need it. Her black hair had a few silver strands scattered throughout. They appeared immediately after the miscarriage. She stood almost six feet with slender, fine bone features.

Although I'd never actually seen her go shopping, she had the latest styles in clothing and shoes. With every outfit she wore either matching or contrasting cheaters hung from a cord around her neck.

I loved her even if she made me look even shorter than my five feet-one, and I couldn't hold a candle to her in looks. I knew no one would throw a bag over my head so they didn't have to look at me.

We didn't have time to finish our coffee before Nathan came in with the dogs. Mine jumped up to meet their friends. I walked over, opened the kitchen door and let them out. Sally had gained weight; I opened the door so she didn't have to squeeze through the doggy door. They would run and wrestle for at least ten minutes.

Before I had a chance to call into the office and talk to Roger Simon, he called me. I answered, put the phone on the counter and turned on the speaker so Amy could hear what he had to say. "I'd ask how the case is going, but I think I know."

"There was nothing in or around the Cadillac. They had even taken the serial numbers off of the engine and the car itself. Not so much as a hair, a thread or a partial fingerprint to be found.

"The truck you think was involved in the murders was found on County Road 153. It had been burned. Same thing, no fingerprints, serial numbers or markings. You can drive out there if you want, but it is all the way out in Franklin County. It has been gone over with a fine tooth comb. I think it would be a waste of time. Tell me what you think."

"Amy and I believe they have punished all the men they had in mind, therefore, they got rid of everything linking them to the killings."

"We are going to spend some time looking for a link between the dead men."

"Sounds like a plan. If you come up with any clues or need anything, let me know."

"By the way, Kate, after the interviews at the excursion boat last night, you are in all of today's papers. There was so much speculation, I had to issue a statement as to why you are once again with the Homicide Unit and who Amy is. Sorry."

Before I could say another word, he hung up.

"Geez, is this ever going to stop?"

"Do you want my honest answer?" She asked. "No, it isn't. You are pretty, nice and married to *THE* Ryan Meade. You are either going to a gallery opening in a stunning dress or dining out with Ryan's clients who always warrant a word or two on the society page.

"Besides, partner, you must admit, for the last few years, we have caught more murders than the police force."

She got up to let the dogs in. We fooled around playing with them for a while before we went to work.

CHAPTER 18

Nine days had passed since the last killing. We attended all of the funerals. The same three men stood outside the door at all of the services. After the first one, we called Roger and told him we needed a surveillance detail to follow the trio, but we didn't want them to be seen.

They were an odd group. Each man stood ramrod straight. They couldn't hide the fact they were armed from seasoned professionals like Amy and me. Each had on a three-piece suit, navy blue with vests and steamed creases in their trousers. Had they not stayed within a foot of one another, they would not have been so noticeable.

The car they arrived and left in had vanity plates; D Lodge. I didn't understand why they would be in a car with a vanity plate. They must not have cared if anyone knew who they were.

Victor Mann's funeral took place at Williamson Funeral Home. Nothing out of the ordinary happened. Mourners came and went. The armed men didn't interact with anyone including the family. We might have another clue. I could hardly wait to track down the owner of the vehicle, a new Cadillac Escalade.

We lingered outside until everyone had taken their seats before we went in separately. Amy sat near the front, behind the extended family. I took a seat near the back.

I didn't see the men. They were either outside or had already left. I couldn't be so bold as to look around for them. I sat quietly. The liturgy went on for at least an hour. The minister asked if anyone in the crowd had a memory or story about Victor they would like to share. The number of people who went to the pulpit shocked me. The man seemed to be well liked by everyone. One person didn't like him; the one who killed him.

To hear the minister, his friends and relatives talk, the man could be up for sainthood. We wandered out the doors with the rest of the crowd and eavesdropped on every conversation we could. The men and their car were gone. I could only hope Roger had a team on them.

We met back at the Rover. "I did notice one thing," Amy said, "it is much less stressful to attend a funeral when you don't know the deceased."

The identical events happened at the other funerals. The same men were there. Dressed the same way and again were gone when the service ended.

The Escalade with the vanity plate; D. Lodge belonged to a company out of Kansas City named Merit Realty. Merit Realty, a shell corporation nested under another shell corporation; Violet's Flowers which led us to Mount James Dirt Bikes and Turtle Dove Books.

Since finding the owner of a shell corporation could

hardly be found under one name, four would be nearly impossible to find.

I knew a little about shell corps. They are set up to specifically hide the identities of their owners. Most only existed on paper. They didn't have to have employees, but most had bank accounts to hide money from illegal sources.

There are many things in life I find either over my head or beyond my scope of understanding. One of them is these corporations. The definition tells you they are mostly set to hide money that's either illegal or someone doesn't want to pay taxes. The entire subject made my head hurt.

We took Friday off. Ryan had Cardinal baseball tickets for the four of us on the third base line. Before the seventh inning stretch, my phone rang. Roger didn't waste words. "There has been a shooting a block from the Riverdale Club. All I know is that there was an auto accident outside and shots fired.

"Sorry to ruin your evening, but I'll meet you there. We will stage on the south side, so come in from Chippewa instead of Chestnut. The local cops are there but there is something about the scene that makes them believe it's your killer."

Again, he hung up before I could ask a question or make a statement. I don't know what caused his lack of manners, but I didn't like it.

Roger and I had been partners for ten years. We worked well together and got to the point where we knew instinctively what to do without talking to one another. This wasn't the same. Maybe the brass were pushing him to find the killers. I didn't know.

The seventh inning went three up and three down as

did the eighth. Amy and I wondered how much we'd be pushing it if we waited until the game was over. Leaving the park and the lot wouldn't be a problem. I had a siren and lights and I wouldn't hesitate to use them.

The score had been tied two to two since the third inning. I whispered to Ryan about the shooting south of downtown. Amy got the call on her radio the same time as I did and was already on her feet.

I told Ryan to finish watching the game, we'd get a ride with a cop. He started to protest. I leaned down, kissed him lightly and said, "We'll catch up with you guys at the grill."

The scene looked like a major event. Lights flashed on top of several police cars. Two ambulances and a firetruck were on the scene when a patrolman by the name of Rick Newman dropped us a block from the center of the mess. We walked in.

We both had to flash badges until we got to Roger Simon who seemed to be heading up the investigation. A bright blue Honda Accord, a black F150 and a white GMC Denali sat nearly on top of one another. They were so mangled I couldn't tell who ran into who. I noticed the men in suits; Secret Service, I thought. Why would they be here?

Roger, although we had been twenty feet away, made it to us in about three steps. "It is Congressman Atticus Riley from East St. Louis. Someone shot him through the window of the car.

"He and an agent were in the front; Riley's wife and two daughters were in the Honda.

"Bystanders said the truck pulled out in front of the congressman's car. The agent driving swerved and ran into the Honda. The only lack of protocol was they let Riley sit in the front seat.

"People came from everywhere to help. But two people on a jock-rocket, no one knows what kind, drove up to the passenger side window and a rider, on the back, emptied a 38 into Riley. Folks were everywhere. No one had an eye on the congressmen, they were too busy trying to get the girls and his wife out of the Honda.

"To make it worse, not only did they let Riley ride in the front, but the youngest girl, just turned sixteen, was at the wheel of the Honda, his wife in the passenger seat and the other daughter, fourteen sat alone in the back. No Secret Service of any kind in her car."

"Sounds like heads will roll," Amy said.

"Is there a description of the shooter or shooters?" I asked.

"No," Roger said, "but this was on the floorboard of the GMC." He handed me a white business card with the words ENUFSENUF in big red letters.

Amy and I stood back for a few moments and tried to assess the scene in front of us. We needed to talk to the driver of the truck who, it appeared, caused the entire accident. I asked one of the cops where we could find them. He pointed toward a woman sitting on the back of an ambulance with its doors open. I asked her, "Is that your truck?"

A pretty Hispanic woman of about forty looked up at me. "Is that your truck," I asked again, looking toward the pile of mangled metal.

"No," she said, "it belongs to my son. My car had a flat tire. He let me use it so I wouldn't be late for work."

"Where do you work?" Amy asked

"At Joy Manor Nursing Home. I'm late, I'll most likely be fired."

"You have worse problems than that," I said.

She covered her face with both hands and began to sob.

Amy took a step in front of me which put her close enough to lay her hand on the crying woman. She led her away from the crowd and had her lean against a car not involved in the ordeal. "Tell me what happened, step by step, everything you can remember."

"I left the house late. I didn't have a chance to put on my eye liner so I put it on at the stop light." She wiped her tears away with the back of her hand and blew her nose on a tissue I saw the ambulance driver give her. "The light must have turned green, the person in the car behind me began to honk his horn. Then the car bumped me. I put my foot on the gas and went on across the intersection.

"The light was not green. It was still red. I ran into that blue car over there."

"Can you tell me what kind of car hit you from behind?"

"No, I was too nervous. I believe I hurt those girls and their mother. Government men were in the other car and in a car behind. There must be a government man involved somehow." She began to cry again.

"Did you hear gunshots?"

She shook her head violently. "No, no," she said, she began to cry again.

"One of those men in the suits pulled me out of the truck and said I was under arrest. They won't let me call my boy."

I handed her my phone. "Call him now.

"What is your name?" I asked.

"Salenna Gomez."

"You wait right here, Mrs. Gomez. It might take a while to sort this out. Are you hurt?"

"No, I don't think so."

We walked over to a group of four men in suits I guessed were Secret Service. "I'm Detective Kate Nash, this is my partner, Detective Amy Perkin. Can anyone tell us what happened?"

"We are handling this case. You two should just run along."

A good looking man in his early thirties stepped forward. "I'm Agent Milord. You'll have to excuse Ritchey. He knows he is about to get his head handed to him, and he is a bit out of sorts.

"We made a mistake letting the Congressman sit in the front seat. The rest of this is not our fault. We had no idea the girls and their mother were behind us."

"Let me get this straight. You had a congressman in a car, taking him somewhere."

"To the airport," one of the others said.

"You let him sit in the front seat. His daughter was the driver of the car right behind you but you didn't know it. And they had no protection."

"That just about covers it, Detective," Milord said.

"Before you dismiss us," I said, "let me give you a few facts. The people who killed Congressman Riley have killed six other people. We thought they were done killing because they stopped for nine days.

"We know now it was to change their MO."

Another agent said, "How do you know it is the same people?"

I took the card out of my pocket and held it out for all to see. "Because of this. It has been at every crime scene in one form or another. Even though I think you were thinking like a bunch of feather heads tonight, you could not have protected your charge. He did something they thought he should be killed for. Once they make that determination, the victim is as good as dead.

"I am actually sorry it happened on, most likely the one and only night you screwed up, but his death was inevitable. Nothing you could have done."

Before any of the men had a chance to speak, Amy said, "The only thing for you to do is to make the best situation you can out of this. We will investigate your man along with the other four and try our best to find out why these men are being murdered.

"Your best bet is to check on Riley's family at the hospital and inform your superiors about the killing. We can take care of the rest."

We turned and walked away.

"What do you think?" I said to Amy.

"I think they are in big trouble, and I don't believe no one saw anything. Lastly, whoever ran into Salenna Gomez and pushed her forward did it on purpose."

We walked up to a group of interested onlookers and Amy shouted, "Anyone know or see what happened here? Any information would be appreciated."

A man of about fifty came over. He stood ram rod straight and wore a jogging suit much too hot for the night. He'd had a recent haircut and I noticed he had a manicure. He pointed to the wreck. "That black truck was at the stoplight over there." Again, he pointed. "I know because I was two cars behind her.

"Somebody in the car between us began to honk like

he wanted the truck to move out of his way. I don't know why he was so anxious because the light was red.

"Next thing I know, the car bumped the truck really hard and the truck went into the intersection."

Amy and I looked at one another. "Do you know where the other car is now?"

The gentleman said the car peeled out of the middle of the accident and took off as fast as he could down Cass. He had to have passed some of the police as he left.

I called one of the CSI crew over. His name tag read Don. "Hey Don, would you get some photos of the back of the truck, where another car hit it?"

Don glanced toward the back of the F150. "Be glad to. Where is the car in question?"

I grinned at him. "That seems to be the question of the hour."

When I turned my attention to the man in the track suit again, he had left. "So much for a helpful concerned citizen," I said. "Did anyone see the car that caused the accident?" I yelled in a voice everyone around us could here.

"Can anyone tell me anything about the car? Color or model or make?"

A man about thirty stepped forward from the crowd. He looked like he might have been down on his luck. His hair needed a good shampoo and I had to take a step back from him because of his body odor. The Nike tee shirt and Levi jeans he wore had once belonged to a much bigger person.

"I got the license plate number," he said. He took a piece of a napkin out of his pocket and handed it to me.

"Sorry it's so messy. It's all I had. If you can't read it, I can tell you what it says."

"No, I think I have it. RTE284. Missouri plate?"

"No, Illinois," he said.

Amy took the paper, walked away and thanked him. I watched her walk over to Roger and hand it to him. He reached for his radio. She came back to us.

"That isn't all I saw," he said, "after the three vehicles hit one another, a motorcycle drove up. I can't tell you what kind it was. It was a jock rocket, if that helps."

"You mean not a well-known brand like a Harley?"

Amy looked from him to me. "A jock rocket, a small bike where the passenger sits behind and above the driver. They are cheap and fast."

"What did the motorcycle driver do?"

"There were two people on the cycle. They both wore black with whole head and face shields. The one in the back got off the bike, walked over to the window of the GMC and nodded yes to the person still on the bike.

"Whoever it was, got back on the bike, behind the driver, took out a gun, leaned down and shot five or six times at the man in the passenger's seat. Then they left. No one seemed to notice them. The driver took off, the front wheel came off of the pavement and they were gone. Just like in a Ninja movie."

After two hours we had a complete story. We talked to several witnesses and as always they all had a little different take on what happened. An older model Toyota Corolla, probably a 2011 hit the black F150 truck forcing it into the intersection where it broadsided the Honda. I found it strange since the Secret Service said the Honda was behind them. I decided they were wrong because they were not paying any attention to the Honda since they had no idea who the occupants were.

The Feds, or at least some of them ran to the congressman. More ran to the Honda carrying the girls and Mrs. Riley. No one ran to help Mrs. Gomez.

My phone rang, Ryan said, "Are you about done or should we go home?"

"Just about done here. It's the ENUFSENUF folks. They changed their MO. Give us ten minutes, we will be there."

We walked back to the group of Feds. We each pulled out a few business cards, passed them out, told them what we thought happened and who was responsible.

They had doubled in number since we saw them earlier. I didn't want to be in their shoes trying to explain how a congressman lost his life on the way to the airport and why they broke the rules.

It sucked to be them.

CHAPTER 19

Mike's Grill sat two blocks East of Lindberg in a plain looking shopping center. There were two anchor stores, a Designer Shoe Warehouse and a Bed, Bath and Beyond. The rest of the stores were specialty shops, Ruth's Gifts and Flowers, Wayne's Tea Shop carrying teas from the world over and my personal favorite, a new age store named, The Purple Frog.

You could park anywhere in the huge lot and walk to the restaurant. Mike's was famous for the kind of food everyone wanted to eat but knew they shouldn't. They served Mac 'n Cheese with five varieties of cheese and baked with a bread crumb topping until the bread and top layer of cheese were crispy.

The Mike Dog hardly fit on the bun. It started with a cheddar and jalapeno brat on a toasted buttered bun. Under the brat they put German style sauerkraut. On top sat onions, chili, relish and cheese melted over the entire sandwich. I got heartburn reading about it on the menu.

My favorite was most likely the healthiest dish in the place. The chicken salad had big chunks of chicken breast, walnuts, grapes, celery, fresh apples and cantaloupe. The dressing tasted like maybe it had both sour cream and mayo. It came with a blueberry muffin and cold strawberry soup.

I didn't care much for beer, but Mike's were served out of a tap in a frosted, nearly frozen mug. They had one kind of beer, Mike's beer. No one complained.

Amy and I ordered the chicken salad. Ryan had a pulled pork sandwich which sat at least five inches high due to the huge amount of Cole slaw on top. Nathan ordered a Mike Dog. Diana, one of the waitresses we knew by name, brought us a pitcher of beer and four mugs while we waited.

Amy and I made a pact on the way over not to talk about the case. We were murdered out for the night. Since we'd agreed to help Roger Simon, murder had dominated our lives.

"You missed a good game," Nathan said.

"We listened to the highlights on the way here. Seems we missed the most exciting part," I said.

A loud noise came from the front of the grill and instinctively Amy and I both stood and put our hands on our guns. The ruckus turned into laughter. We sat down.

Ryan put his hand on mine. "I'll be glad when this case is over. You two are much too stressed. Any leads?"

I moved my hand on top of his and said, "We don't want to talk about it. All we want to do is overeat, drink too much beer and go to bed without murder being the first subject on our minds, right, Amy?"

"Right," she said.

My phone rang, Roger Simon, the caller ID read. The best laid plans, as they say.

"What's up, Roger?" I asked.

"I thought I'd give you a heads up about the car that started the crash. It's a 2012 Toyota Corolla, reported stolen three days ago from O'Fallon, Illinois. It was found abandoned on Rogers Road in Highland. The Illinois State Police are taking it in to go over it. That's all I have."

"Thanks, Roger."

CHAPTER 20

Nathan and Amy took my car home and I rode with Ryan. His jet-black Ford F150, 4x4 sat so high off the ground, I had to use the chrome side bars to step up and the inside fraidy handle to swing into the seat.

The night had turned cool. I could smell fall in the air. We heard the dogs barking in excitement from two blocks away. "I guess we'd better prepare ourselves," I said. "We are about to be mauled by canines."

For a good five minutes Chili ran from Ryan to me and back. Our gentleman, Axel, sat quietly by the couch waiting for an invitation to come over. Once we acknowledged him, he wagged and wiggled like a puppy.

Ryan grabbed a small handful of dog treats from the dog shaped cookie jar in the kitchen, and we all four headed outside. Axel caught a Frisbee several times while Chili laid on my knees and watched.

"Your turn, little girl," he called to her, and instantly, I no longer held her attention. She ran through her commands with Ryan. She sat and got rewarded with a piece of a treat. The same thing happened when she sat up on her back legs, laid down, rolled over and stayed on command.

It ended her little show. She ran over to me and begged to take back her spot on my lap.

"Want a glass of wine?"

"No. Truthfully, I'd like a hot bath and a good night's sleep."

Ryan grinned at me. "Want some company?"

I stood and kissed him. "Sure."

"You stay here and relax; I'll go up and get the bath ready. Give me ten minutes and then come up."

When he went into the house, he took the dogs with him. I sat in the silence and tried to clear my mind of jock rockets, dead bodies, and murderers.

I stayed outside enjoying the cool air and silence, much longer than ten minutes, I knew.

Upstairs, Chili had gone to sleep on my pillow and Axel curled up in his bed by the window. He looked relaxed, but I knew he would not go to sleep until both Ryan and I were safely tucked in.

I took off my clothes and the rubber band out of my hair and slipped on a robe. The inside of the bathroom had been turned into a wonderland.

Bubbles were all the way to the top of the huge claw foot tub. A lit candle graced every surface, and two full wine glasses sat on the edge of the tub. Ryan had already climbed in. I dropped my robe and got in with my back to his chest and leaned against him.

We laughed and talked and sipped our wine until the water turned cold. I hadn't been so relaxed since Amy and I agreed to help Roger Simon while the pandemic raged through the world.

An hour later we were ready for a good night's sleep.

CHAPTER 21

I had had two cups of latte and started slathering my second bagel with blueberry cream cheese when I heard Amy and the dogs coming in through the garage. She closed the garage door behind her.

"Hey, sleepy head," I said to her when she walked into the kitchen.

"I know, and boy did it feel good."

"The results of a relaxing soak in the tub and a glass of wine." She nodded toward the file folder on the counter. "What do you have there?"

"Nathan had Jacob make a spread sheet of the victims. It has space for every detail of their lives he could think of. If we take the time to fill in all of the blanks, we will know if these men have anything in common."

The entire time she talked, the dogs danced and chased one another playfully. "Time to put the big guys outside," I said and looked at Chili. "Want to go outside or come with me." She ran over to my leg and sat up on her hind legs for me to pick her up.

"What about you, little boy," Amy said to Diggers. "I think he is going with us."

We had a habit of locking the office door and turning off our private server and the satellite connection every night when we were done with our day's work. Jacob had set up a system for us to access the FBI, CIA and to the Homeland Security files we needed to do our background checks and now to delve into the lives of the men who were killed for what seemed like no apparent reason.

Ryan and Jacob told us we only had a middle level clearance to these agencies; Amy and I didn't question it. We only knew we had information so fast, sometimes Roger Simon had dropped by to have us run a check on a possible suspect.

It took a good ten minutes to turn on all the machines, links and monitors. We each had a thirty inch screen on our desks, which also projected onto fifty-four inch ones we could both see. To the left the screen showed the cameras around the house. We knew if anyone came within a quarter of a mile of the office without having to look outside of the room.

The security screen had to be the largest. I didn't know the exact size but I guessed over sixty inches. There were several small screens inside the big one. We could see the backyard, all four sides of the house, the driveway and a block each way up and down the street.

Some people might have found it overkill, but once a man dug under the fence, let Chili out, climbed over the fence and threw a bomb into the sliding glass door shattering the glass.

It didn't help that my mother, well, the lady who pretended to be my mother, and my Uncle Dominic

DeMarco ran the mafia on the upper East coast for forty years. They were both spending, what I hoped, was life in prison.

My twin sister took over the *family business* and in the last few years had turned it into a lucrative enterprise. There were skeptics around who not only didn't believe a word of it but held grudges against Dominic and his sister.

"Are you ready?" Amy asked, "If so let's get started. These men must not be as squeaky clean as they seem."

We worked until noon. I'd run Victor Mann, Dennis Small and Kendal Mardell through CODIS, the FBI database, CIA, and the watchlist on Homeland Security's site.

Amy did the same for Benjamin Highland and Congressman Atticus Riley.

All of it...dead ends.

We fixed ham and Swiss sandwiches on rye bread and frozen French fries. They cooked in the microwave in four minutes. After grabbing a Pepsi from the fridge we went outside with all the dogs. The big dogs were sound asleep in the sun. The little dogs went to romp on them and wake them up.

"What do we know now we didn't know this morning?" I asked.

"That Benjamin Highland and Atticus Riley both lost kids. Highland boy's health was so compromised, he couldn't move, but didn't actually die until five years later.

"Atticus Riley had a seven year old girl. She was caught in the crossfire of two rival gangs while walking to a car her father had sent for her. She laid in a coma for 6 years."

I took a bite of my sandwich and then said, "My three had family who lingered on life support also. Victor Mann had a brother. They were in business together and he had a stroke. Victor let him live nine years until someone intervened.

"Dennis Small had a sister who had some disease. The files were vague about what it was. She lived 7 years with a feeding tube and unable to move more than her little finger.

Our coach, Kendall Mardell, wouldn't stop practice one hot day for a junior, who didn't feel well, to get a drink of water. The kid had a heat or sun stroke and didn't wake up again. He died four years later after being in a coma the entire time. The parents sued the coach and the school. After the kid's parents sued the school and won, they took their other children and left the state."

"What year was that?"

"As far as I can tell, 2013."

"They are either the unluckiest group of men I've ever heard of, or maybe in someway they had a hand in the act that put their relatives in a coma. Other than the coach, I can't find that anyone else was responsible. Just normal living and dying," I said.

We went back to the office and this time all four dogs went along. They all had their favorite places to lay. Axel preferred the bare floor as did Sophie. Diggers and Chili had small beds. Most of the time the two little ones shared the same bed.

Amy began to look for the boy who died at the school where Mardell taught and coached in 2013. "Here, I found it. Seems it was the story of the decade. The boy's name, Taylor Martin Peterman, age sixteen."

She put the article up on the screen and read it aloud anyway.

The headline read…

Freshman Taylor Martin Peterman has heat stroke.

Varsity football coach, Kendal Mardell, said the school was very careful with the players because of the extreme heat. Football practice had been moved from ten a.m. to eight a.m. so as to protect the players from the mid-day heat.

Mardell said Peterman had gone for a drink not ten minutes before he asked again. Coach told him to wait until the scrimmage ended.

A few minutes later, Peterman lay on the field unconscious. An ambulance arrived a few minutes later but the EMTs were not able to revive Peterman.

Five days later

Taylor Peterman remains in a coma at St. Luke's Hospital ICU. His parents John and Louise Peterman say the story they are hearing from the other players and the one told by Coach Mardell are not the same.

The other players said coach called the players who stopped for water, fairies, girls, babies, weak and pansies as well as names I cannot repeat here.

It has been a month since the tragedy. Doctors say the chances of the boy regaining consciousness are slim.

The Peterman's filed a multimillion dollar lawsuit against the school, the school system and against Kendal Mardell.

Seven years later:

Taylor Martin Peterman, the young football player from Jordan High died today of a heat stroke he suffered in 2013.

In 2016 the Peterman's filed a lawsuit against the school and the coach. They settled for an undisclosed amount.

Details of the boy's funeral are pending.

"I could see why someone would want to kill the coach. What he did was uncalled for and cruel. Many people think to teach by degrading is the way to go," I said.

Amy took the story down and looked toward me. "I believe it's a horrible coincidence all of the victims had a person in a coma in common. I guess it is more common than I thought. I doubt it was the reason they were murdered.

"It would involve too many people. Also, I don't know how they would know one another unless all of the coma victims were in the same long-term facility. Before I let this go, I'm going to take a look and see what I can find."

"It's worth a try," I said. "I'll start looking into who might have gone to church together. Or they could have belonged to the same club. Maybe they knew one another through their wives."

We were quiet the rest of the day. Amy researched her theories and I searched mine.

Seven hours later, we still had nothing.

CHAPTER 22

Ryan stood in the kitchen with my cell phone in his hand. "Hi, you two must have been engrossed in your work. I called to see if there was anything I could get for supper and no one answered."

When I reached around to check my back pocket where I usually housed my phone, it was no longer there. I pointed to his hand. "Where did you find it?" I asked.

"On the counter." He walked over, reached for my back pocket and slipped it in where it belonged as he kissed me lightly on the lips.

"My, I meant to leave early," Amy said. "Nathan is cooking his famous Chili Rellenos. My only job was to pick up beer and chips." She told her dogs to go the car and blew us a kiss at the door.

Ryan went upstairs to shower and change into dress clothes. He had a banquet at the Convention Center. Sometimes I went along, but this was the closing of a show of products he and six or seven other companies put together to keep homes safe.

Meade Security didn't usually deal with home security. They handled the big guys: stadiums, school districts, manufacturing plants, art galleries and high-end jewelry stores, to name a few.

Ring, Blink, and SimpliSafe opened the door for every home owner to have a security system. He wasn't interested in dealing with individual homeowners, but he wasn't against opening a division and staffing it with a crew who didn't mind it.

CHAPTER 23

After the ham sandwich and French fries in the late afternoon, I wasn't hungry for dinner. I made microwave popcorn, took a big glass of water and another of red wine and went up to the bedroom.

Ryan and I had decorated it together. The walls were light grey. Instead of curtains or drapes we had blinds in a darker shade. The Berber carpet had black, white, dark and light greys and a touch of red. Our king-size bed had four body pillows across the head board, which was Bamboo, and multicolor accent pillows matching the colors in the rug.

Something about the room helped me relax as soon as I stepped in. After a shower and changing into pj's I settled in. I watched one of my favorite old movies, *Someone to Watch Over Me,* staring Tom Berenger, Mimi Rogers and Lorraine Bracco. Mimi was once married to Tom Cruise in the late eighties. I could never wrap my mind around it.

Dr. Dane Willis, the medical examiner, called right in the middle of my film and said he wanted to see us. He said he had a major clue and it had been missed because he'd been on vacation and three other doctors rotated through his position to keep up. I told him Amy and I would be there by eleven.

Ryan didn't wake when I got dressed and ready to leave. I dressed in a pair of worn Lucky jeans, a long sleeve tangerine colored tee with a scooped neck. To dress myself up a little I added a diamond pendant Ryan gave me for our anniversary and earrings to match.

Before I slipped on a navy blue double-breasted jacket, I stuffed my Glock into my waist band at the small of my back.

I left my hair for last. It commanded a lot of attention. It matched the red-orange hue of Lucille Ball's hair, but mine was natural. My light blue eyes and light skin made an impression on people who doubted it a color I had at birth. Showing each skeptic a baby picture would have taken too much time so I merely smiled and moved on. Mostly due to the thickness and curls, I gathered it at the back of my neck and held it with a scrunchie.

I went quietly through my morning routine and headed downstairs. I wondered why the dogs were not in the room with us. The answer to my question came when I went down the stairs and saw Amy, who sat at the bar and smiled at me. "Did you get the call; Dr. Willis wants us to come to the morgue?"

"I did. The part where he said he had a clue intrigued me," she said.

Amy looked especially beautiful in the morning light in a teal blue silk blouse, tan slacks and no jacket. "That's your color, you know?" I told her. "Are you going without a jacket today?"

"I thought I would. Sometimes the shoulder holster

rubs me until I'm sore. Besides, I love it when people look at my gun before they look at me. It gives a whole new meaning to social distancing."

I laughed, took my jacket off. She was correct about the jacket. It would be hot the next three days, then rain and a cold front would come through and a coat would be a must.

"Let me get my latte and a bagel, and I'll be ready to go."

She went to the microwave and the toaster oven. She came back with my breakfast. "Let's go," she said. "We can take your car; I'll drive so you can eat."

"Well drive slow. I want to make sure my breakfast is down and settled in case Willis has something gross to show us."

The morgue, which used to be in the bottom of St. Mary's Hospital was now housed in its own building across town. I didn't have to worry about Amy driving slow. The traffic took care of it. We were stop and go the entire twenty-something miles.

The doors at the morgue were always locked and it brought the same old joke to mind every time. *It was kept locked because people were dying to get in.*

Before I had a chance to say it out loud, Amy said it first and then said, "I sometimes think about your joke when I go past a cemetery and I blame it on you. If Nathan ever leaves me, it will be all your fault- you and your dumb jokes."

A man I hadn't seen before opened the door and escorted us in. The second the cold air in the room reached my face, I turned serious.

Dr. Willis came out and suggested we go into his office. "For one thing, it is warmer in there." He wore green scrubs and cloth slippers over his shoes. He took off his gloves as we followed him. He tossed them into a waste can in the corner of a hallway.

He motioned to two chairs across from his desk and said, "Please have a seat. I know you will be upset about this, but with my time off and three different doctors handling the bodies, I'm afraid no one noticed this until I returned yesterday and read all of the reports."

Amy gave me a quick glance and I knew she thought the same thing I did. *Get on with it.*

He opened his desk drawer and brought out a large manilla envelope. He poured its contents on his desk.

A large packet of papers fell out. "I think this is what binds your victims together. When I read all of the reports, I realized the names were familiar.

"I took the liberty of doing a little research. There was a famous serial killer some years back; thirty years ago, to be exact. He was arrested, tried and let go because some of the jurors said they didn't think he was the killer.

"The men, whose murders you are investigating were on that jury. It was quite an ordeal. The story earned first page status in the newspapers for months. The man's fingerprints were at the crime scenes. Three eye witnesses identified him, yet five of the twelve thought him innocent. No one knows why but somehow those five talked the others into changing their votes.

"After two full weeks of deliberation, they found him innocent and the authorities were forced to release him. The judge acted like he was horrified. He polled the jury and let them go. The prosecution wanted a mistrial, but there were no known improprieties attributed to the defense or the prosecution."

I couldn't believe it. "So do you think these were revenge killings, Dr. Willis?"

Before the doctor had time to answer, Amy interrupted and asked. "What happened to the killer? Is he still alive?"

Dr. Willis took a blue towel from off the top of his desk, wiped his glasses and his face. "No, the first few weeks he holed up in the old Belle Hotel downtown. People from all walks of life picketed and harassed him. Everyone knew he was the killer.

"Some of the relatives of the victims were inconsolable.

"To this day, there has been speculation the jury was paid off by someone. How much they were paid and who figured it all out has always been a mystery. Many believe the judge had to be paid off too. He knew the man had killed those people; he would have been within his rights to overturn their verdict and put the man back on trial, but he didn't.

"In the middle of the night, the next week, he packed a bag, walked to Union Station with a ticket to Chicago in his billfold.

"He didn't make it. Someone, or several someone's, gunned him down. In the suitcase he was carrying were souvenirs from the killings. From what they found, they were able to identify eleven more victims they didn't know of before.

"No one believed Malloy had any money. But within three years, the men on the jury who were responsible for his release all came into money. I think one bought a furniture store, another one a chain of restaurants, and the younger ones went to college. If my memory serves me, one became a high school football coach and another a financial advisor."

He pushed the papers back into the envelope. "I can do you one better than that. I'm a bit of a history buff. I followed the trial and these are my notes. They include the names of the people who were killed by John Michael Malloy, the accused.

"Actually, I recognize all the names. I did their autopsies. At least it is a start for you. I didn't spend much time studying the jury. I was more interested in those who he killed. He kept me busy for years.

"Also, it happened over thirty years ago. The rest of what you need is probably in this packet." He stood. "I really must go back to work now."

He turned and walked out of the office. Amy and I sat quietly for a few minutes, trying to absorb the entire implication of what he told us.

CHAPTER 24

The excitement between Amy and I was palpable in the room. We practically ran to the car. Once we were in, I turned toward Amy. "Open the envelope and let's take a better look."

"You bet," she said as she opened the flap and let the papers slide out onto her hand. "All of the dead men had to either be on the jury or have something to do with this ordeal. We now know for a fact they all met their demise for the same reason."

I looked up from studying the papers in the envelope. "We don't have enough information. Let's get back to the office so we can do some research of our own."

We didn't talk much on the way home. Amy took the time to read the papers and I made up scenarios in my mind even without facts. I knew I needed to stop.

I believe it's a Universal Law, when I am excited about a project, events jump in my way. First an accident on 270 held us up for nearly an hour. Next, the low fuel light went on in my car and we had to stop for gas.

It didn't end there. All four dogs were in the house needing attention when we arrived. While I went outside with the four of them, Amy made sure they had fresh water. They knew we would take them to the office with us so they settled down in no time at all.

Amy, who is always hungry yet looked like she never ate, reminded me it was after two pm and we hadn't had lunch or even a sip of water since before ten.

I searched the fridge and came up with leftover pizza and spinach and artichoke dip. Amy got chips from the pantry. We warmed the food, grabbed a couple of bottles of Diet Pepsi from the drink refrigerator and headed for the office.

The dogs happily trotted behind us. When we settled down to do some research. We discussed where to start.

Amy typed the name, John Michael Malloy, into one of the computers and changed the settings so it projected onto the biggest screen on the wall in front of us. As Google always does, it told us how many mentions of the name and how long it took the search engine to find them.

443,983 files in .0034 seconds. I found it overwhelming.

The picture of Malloy showed a young man in his late twenties or early thirties. The black and white picture showed he had dark hair, dark eyes and dark skin. We didn't think him to be Black or Hispanic, only dark complected. The photo came from a newspaper article and the photo lacked definition. The date on the article said January 3, 1992.

Hollister, Missouri police arrested a suspect in the killings of Danny Ransom, Mark O'Neal, James

Adamson, Latisha Sears and Elizabeth (Betty) Smith.

The authorities from St. Peters, St. Charles, Hollister, St. Louis County and City along with members of the FBI helped with the apprehension.

Malloy was found hiding in the basement of a vacant house in a rural area. He was taken without incident.

We will update this story as more information becomes available.

I crossed my arms over my chest. "That was a lot of nothing."

Amy smiled. "We have over 443,000 more chances to find what we need."

By the time Ryan came home, we knew much more about the killer and his victims. Malloy followed his victims, sometimes for weeks. In an interview with police, he related he didn't have a happy life. He had a goal. He wanted to follow someone around and see how they lived: what they ate and drank, if they went to church, were they happy in their marriage. By the time he killed his victim, he knew everything about them.

He said had he found any one of them to be truly happy he would not have killed them. If he found them unhappy, by his standard, he would murder them and move on to someone else.

These murders happened over several years and nothing about them matched the ones years before. After Malloy killed three men, he began making mistakes. He left fingerprints on James Adamson and Betty Smith.

He murdered them all the same way: two shots to the chest and one to the head. Anyone with any training in firearms, including the authorities, knew standard teaching practice included the words two to the chest and one to the head.

After the three men, he switched to women. He told the FBI, he found it reasonable if men weren't happy, maybe women were. His standards, as they were, didn't change. The women had to die if they weren't happy.

The articles, as time went forward, had many more facts and clues. It convinced them John Michael Malloy indeed was a serial killer. Once the gun became a positive match for all of the victims, more bodies were found shot with the same gun. After his death, evidence led police to add eleven more bodies to his count. They, however, were not all shot. Some were knifed, strangled and tortured.

Malloy spent nearly three years in jail before the prosecution knew they had all the proof they needed to convict him. Jury selection began in September of 1995.

Ryan knocked softly on the office door. All four dogs jumped to their feet, wagged their tails and headed for the door. "You ladies plan to work all night?"

"No," we said in unison. Amy added, "If I read anything else about this serial killer, I won't sleep tonight."

By this time, Ryan had knelt down on the rug and petted each dog in turn. "What serial killer?" he asked.

Amy and I had shut down the computers and were out of our chairs. I told Ryan, "Let's talk about all of it tomorrow. I agree with Amy. If I don't get my mind on something else, I'll be up all night."

CHAPTER 25

Amy, Diggers and Sally left shortly after Ryan came home. I could still feel the fluttering in my stomach. A serial killer, who killed people he stalked and proved, in his own mind, were unhappy. Once he made up his mind, he shot them. Over the course of several years he killed without being caught.

Once he resided in jail, Mitchell Wilhoite, the St. Louis District Attorney at the time, didn't rush the case. According to what I read, he turned over every rock, questioned every witness and searched the killer's home before he decided to take the man to trial. He stayed in jail for three and a half years before they finally paneled a jury.

The State wanted the death penalty. If found guilty, the defense wanted life in prison without possibility of parole. One side or the other needed to convince the jury who would make the ultimate decision. I had never served on a jury. When I worked as a cop in St. Louis, I wasn't eligible. No one wanted me in a death penalty case anyway because I didn't believe in it. In the course of my career, I hadn't had to kill anyone. Oh, I came close a few times, even shot a man once.

Ryan stood on the far side of the counter leaning on a cabinet. "Kate, are you there? I thought you didn't want to address the case anymore tonight. I can see on your face and the deepness of the lines on your forehead it's what you're thinking about."

I walked around the counter and hugged him. "You're right. I need to stop. Let's cook something."

"Good idea. How about spaghetti Carbonara? You make the salad and butter the garlic bread for the oven and I'll make the pasta."

Ryan loved to cook. More times than not, he would have a fabulous dinner waiting when I came in from work. Working with the St. Louis Homicide Division and the murders, meant I no longer had regular hours. Except when Nathan and Ryan barbecued, we mostly had carry out or carry in. The food from Ryan's high end dinner spots topped anything we could cook for ourselves.

Even though I had an interest in Ryan's work, we hadn't talked about it for weeks. I tried to keep up with what famous people visited the restaurants and any news about his crew. Over the years I had met and learned to love each one of them. We hadn't talked about him for weeks. "How's everyone at work," I asked. "I miss knowing what is happening. I'll be glad when we find the killer. Remind me, if Roger ever asks me again to work for him, the answer is no."

The smell of pancetta cooking flowed through the entire room. "I second that. As a matter of fact, he has got to have enough detectives to take over, why are you still on the case?"

I stopped chopping vegetables and put my knife down. His back was to me. I sneaked up behind him and slid my arms around him. "You know how I am. I started this, and now I need to finish it. Amy feels the same way. But I won't tell him yes again."

He turned around and kissed me on top of the head. "Stop messing with the cook or this will never be done."

To make the dressing for the salad of romaine, iceberg and red lettuce, along with chopped carrots, broccoli, cauliflower, scallions and tomatoes, I squeezed a fresh lemon into a small bowl, added a little olive oil, salt, pepper, minced garlic, a touch of honey and poured it over the salad before I tossed it. I divided it into two wooden bowls and sat them on the table with the silverware, plates and napkins. By the time I was finished, Ryan sat a huge bowl of Carbonara in the middle of the table.

Our evening together relieved me of the tension I'd had all day. I told hm about the case and the jury. He shared with me, Bobbie and his wife Marie, were expecting their first child in the spring. He transferred Randy Duke to Joplin to oversee a residential store the company bought there to compete with the other home security brands.

He said he went up with Bobby and let him pick out a house to rent. Since he didn't know the town, he paid six months rent on it. The plan was to give Bobby and Marie a chance to settle into the town and find the neighborhood they wanted to live in.

The stress lifted out of both of us and seemed to disappear as dinner went on. We washed and dried the dishes and Ryan suggested, "It is sixty outside. Let's walk down to Ted Drew's."

I patted my stomach. "I couldn't eat another bite."

He looked down at the four eyes intently staring up at us. "They are hungry. At least they think they are. This weather will be gone next week. I doubt we'll want to walk in the twenty degree weather next week."

As I looked down, I said, "Who wants to go for a walk?"

They ran in circles, then went to the garage where we stowed their harnesses.

Usually we couldn't see many stars due to the city lights. Tonight they were shining brightly in spite of the man-made glow around us.

When we had Axel on a lead, people had different reactions. Some walked by him without changing their path but didn't look his way. Others cut him a wide berth. At Ted Drew's, we bought each dog a small cone and sat at an outside table, each of us holding one so they could eat.

Axel lost all interest in his cone and began to look around. The hair stood up on the back of his neck and a low growl escaped him. "What's wrong, fella?" Ryan asked.

The dog, who had been sitting on the far side of Ryan, stood and walked to my side of the table. He had his back to me and looked even more menacing than before. I rubbed his back but I couldn't calm him down.

I picked up Chili, and Ryan tried to get Axel's attention from something behind us. We neither saw nor heard a noise, yet the dog began to pull Ryan away from the table. What happened next, I'd only seen in the movies. The roar of an engine became loud as a truck ran through the parking lot, bounced off of a sign pole and drove straight into the table where seconds earlier my loving husband had sat.

Ryan dropped Axel's lead and ran toward the vehicle. Inside sat an older gentleman, either dead or knocked out. His head rested on the steering wheel which caused the horn to sound constantly. Ryan gently moved him. The man's head flipped back and would have gone over completely behind him had there not been a rest on the seat to stop it.

Someone yelled, "Call the police!"

Ryan didn't look up. He appeared to be looking for a pulse. Two more people screamed, "Call the police!"

After the third time, I said, "I am the police."

I had momentarily been stunned, and the screaming and yelling brought me back to the present. Chili still rested in my arms. Some of the people moved back away from the truck which spewed smoke, radiator fluid and the smell of gunpowder from the air bags. Ryan had deflated them with his knife to move the man off the horn.

He had dropped Axel's leash, but the dog didn't think of going anywhere. He stood as close to Ryan as he could, his back leaning on Ryan's calf. I sat Chili down beside him. "Watch Chili," I said to my German Shepard. "Don't let her go anywhere. Take her to the table."

Axel picked up his little sister's lead with his teeth and pulled her toward the far side of the table. He laid down, pulled Chili closer to him and put his head down. Never once did he let go of her lead. No one would go near him. When Axel had a job to do, nothing could grab his attention away from his chore.

Once I saw they were both settled, I took out my cell

phone and dialed 9 1 1. "This is Detective Nash, badge 1 4 2 3. Send a team to the corner of Delmar and Forest Park, near the Cheshire Inn and behind Ted Drew's. There has been an accident. Also, send the patrol cars closest to our location.

"Copy Captain Simon and give him this report. There has been an accident. One fatality."

Two things happened nearly immediately. I could hear sirens and my phone rang. Roger Simon hadn't wasted any time.

I told him what I knew, which didn't amount to much. Ryan had disappeared. I assumed he followed the truck tracks back to the original point where the accident began.

I really didn't need to check for a pulse. Ryan had already checked the man and nodded to me he hadn't survived. Enough dead bodies had crossed my path in the past years, I knew one when I saw it. He came back through the bushes and shook his head no. "The tracks went back to a stop sign two streets over. No sign of a disruption and no witnesses visible." Once he pulled the man off of the steering wheel and leaned him away, I could see the cause of death. A butcher knife stuck out of the man's chest around the area of his heart. Blood soaked his white shirt, hands, and the seat. The knife pinned a note to the man's chest, *Enuf's Enuf.* Written on a piece of lined notebook paper in black magic marker.

And I'd thought the killing stopped after the auto crash downtown. I had to stop letting these little delays sway me to think this serial killer would lay down his weapons.

Amy and Nathan were there within ten minutes. She

didn't say anything, she looked at the body and looked at me, then went off in the direction Ryan had gone.

The medical examiner didn't come. He sent the coroner. It would do. We only needed someone to pronounce the man dead so we could move him around, search him for clues and transport him to the morgue. The Medical Examiner, Dr. Dane Willis would be with him soon enough.

I wanted the knife gone over with a fine-toothed comb as soon as possible. Before they took it to the lab, I checked the brand. Mercer showed proximately on the handle, stamped into the stainless steel shaft.

One of the CSI techs came up to me. "The man's name is Darren Reynolds, age seventy-two, the manner of death is murder. The method of death is a stab wound through the heart. Whoever killed him knifed him from the back. I'd venture to say the perp was already in the truck and reached around to kill him."

"By the brand of the knife, I'd say the killer knew his way around a kitchen."

"Dr. Willis will fill you in more when he gets him on the table in the morning. We are done here. If you have seen enough, we will take him away and tow the truck to impound for someone to look it over."

"That's great," I said. "We will be glad to go home ourselves."

"Be careful," he said. I didn't recognize him. His name tag read Logan Dean.

I went over to the dogs. Axel looked relaxed, yet had not taken Chili's leash out of his mouth. Chili was sound asleep lying on his front legs, he had his head lightly resting on her. Someone came up behind me: Amy. "Does the name of the victim sound familiar to you?"

"No, should it?"

"Yes, he was one of the jurors," she replied.

"Wonderful. I guess I was naïve to believe they would only kill six of them. They are going for all twelve. In the morning we should call the others and warn them. Maybe we should have extra protection for the rest of the jurors until we figure this out. Amy and Nathan went home. They offered us a ride but we declined. We didn't get our walk in earlier. Axel's hair still bristled on the back of his neck. Chili had no idea what she missed. She merely slept on our boy until we told her otherwise.

CHAPTER 26

The grandfather clock in the living room struck three as we came in the night before. The dogs were exhausted and hadn't had their regular dinner. They hadn't even gotten to finish their promised treats at the custard shop.

After the animals were taken care of and we'd both showered and brushed our teeth, we didn't talk. I fell asleep immediately. Axel made an unusual noise a couple of hours later. It awoke me and I laid still and quiet for a long time until I made up my mind he was in the middle of a dream.

Ryan breathed slow and steady beside me. I got up to use the bathroom and had plans to go down to the office and work on the case. My body had different ideas and neither Ryan nor I woke up before nine.

The dogs were both asleep. The big shock came when I moved my leg and it bumped Axel. To my knowledge, he had never tried to sleep in the bed before. Chili, as always slept under the covers about half way down the bed between hubby and me.

Instead of Axel waking up and being shy because he knew he shouldn't be in our bed, he wagged his tail, got up and plopped down right next to me with his head on my chest. My heart told me not to scold him but to hug him and let it be.

My cell phone rang at ten. Ryan had showered and gone downstairs with the dogs. I hadn't managed to get dressed yet. "Hi Amy. Did you sleep as late as we did?"

"Yes. Just a heads up, we are on the way over. I guess you've heard the news," she said with an edge in her voice.

"What news? I don't have the TV on."

"No, not that news. The news that Nathan and Ryan want to split us up today and accompany us to visit the surviving jurors."

I laughed, "You're kidding, right?"

"Wish I was. Actually, I'm kind of insulted. I've been a detective for many years and this is the first time someone thought I needed a babysitter. Just wanted to give you a heads up. Didn't want you blindsided like I was."

She hung up before I could say another word.

Ryan still didn't have much to say. I grabbed my clothes and headed for the shower. I chose a pair of navy blue Yoga pants, a long sleeve blue and white checked button-up shirt with a winged collar and Hoka tennis shoes.

Usually I left my Glock on the top of the refrigerator, but we had strayed from our routine the night before. The gun ended up on the night stand on my side of the bed. I didn't bother with a jacket or a holster. I stuck the weapon in the waist band at the small of my back. No one could see it unless they were

the back row of spectators and looked relaxed with his arms crossed over his chest and a Cardinal's baseball hat pulled low on his head.

Ryan said, "It's difficult to see much of him. He appears calm and relaxed considering he is watching the police and CSI scrape body off the pavement."

"Yes," I said. "The Congressman fell out of the car when the perps on the motorbike emptied twelve shells into him and the car."

We went through the hundreds and hundreds of descriptions we had of the killers and the motor bike.

Over and over again we thought we saw the same man. He always leaned on a car or truck as far away as he could and still have an unobstructed view. He had the same stance in every picture. His clothes were always different except for the red Cardinal hat. Had it not been for it, we might not have noticed him.

"It was money. They were killed because of money. The answer is always money," Nathan said. "Amy told me after the trial several of them seemed to have more money. Some of the jurors were down right poor. Suddenly they each had enough money to follow a dream."

"We need to find out where they got it. Did someone in the killer's family offer the jurors large sums of money to let him go?"

I stood and stretched. "The judge had to have been paid off. There is no way, with all of the evidence against the killer, he would have let the jury go without admonishing them. I went through the papers on the desk until I found the what I wanted. "Here it is, Judge Markus Jerome. According to the information I found on him, he retired after the trial. Quit law altogether.

We will have to look up what happened to him."

Amy added, "When I was a street cop in Chicago, a killer who had connections to the mob was acquitted. There were eye-witnesses. The judge called a mistrial, held the jury in contempt until he got to the bottom of it.

"Seems only one juror was at fault. He had a deposit of fifty-thousand dollars into his checking account three days before the jury went into deliberation.

"The killer, who happened to be in his twenties, was the son of a rich land developer. They retried the case and found the man guilty. The juror was arrested for tampering.

"I didn't know until it happened that perjury is a felony in the United States. The guy got five years, plus he lost everything, including the fifty-k."

Nathan stood when Amy did. "Do you realize we have been at this for hours. How about a break and some lunch? We can order in."

By then we were all on our feet and the dogs, knowing something was up, ran to the office door. As I opened it to let them out, I turned around and said, "How about good old-fashioned burgers, fries and milk shakes from Steak 'n Shake? Let's go there. It will take too long for delivery. I'd feel horrible if someone else died while I chowed down."

"You are probably right," Ryan said. "We have already spent hours bringing Nathan and me up to speed about the case."

The dogs were ready for a break as was my butt. Sitting was never my favorite pastime. One of the reasons I wanted to be a PI included following people. For some reason I never considered a stake-out sitting down.

Within a half hour we had lunch in front of us at a corner booth at the restaurant on Halls Ferry Road. I said to the others, "It would take a lot of cash to pay off twelve people. I don't know how many alternates there were, but they would have to get money also.

"After thirty-years, what could have come up to make whoever paid them off decide to kill them? Think maybe someone had a guilty conscience and was going to tell, so he began killing them all?"

Nathan took a big bite of a double cheeseburger and sat it back on his plate. "I believe at least one, and maybe more, of the people have been bleeding the killer dry. Even a small amount over thirty years is a lot of money."

Amy said, "Should we start with the other jurors and warn them or look for a connection between the killer and one of the jurors?"

"I say let's stop the killings by talking to all the other jurors. After all, it is what we started out to do this morning," Ryan said.

"I have the list in my notebook. The thing we don't know is if they are still at the same addresses and how we will be received. You know they will realize we know something has gone bad when they see us at their door," Amy said.

We finished lunch. Amy and Nathan took three jurors and two alternates. We did the same. Ryan and I headed out. Nathan and Amy were on their way to our house to get their dogs and take them home.

Time had passed, but not enough for any of us to forget why we bought the trained dogs. Alarms and cameras were not good enough. There had been no break-ins since Sally and Axel joined our families.

My mind went to home. I never worried about Axel. Sometimes I thought he was smarter than some people I know. Truth is, trained dogs have a single-minded purpose. If they are given a command, they follow it.

One of my worries was put to rest at the training facility. "What happens if someone throws poisoned food over the fence? The dogs would eat it and anyone could come in, not only that, we would lose our dogs."

The retired army major, now trainer, asked us to watch. He put a treat down in front of Axel. The dog ignored it. Then he put a beef patty down. Again, Axel would not touch it. "The only problem I can see," he said, "is what is going to keep the dachshund from eating it. We think we have worked out the answer.

"Chili won't eat the treat if Axel says no. Then he will pick it up in his teeth and drop it in this container. The lid closes and opens when he puts his foot on the switch at the bottom. Let me demonstrate."

A door opened and a cute young beagle came trotting out. He sat by the trainer's leg. "Okay, this is how it will work."

"Axel. No treats. Guard Ralphie." Treats and snacks sailed over the fence. Ralphie headed toward one of them as fast as he could run. Axel ran in front of the puppy and put a paw on his back and growled. The puppy began to go toward the treats anyway. Axel laid on the dog. I noticed he didn't lay hard. He more like tented the dog.

This time when Axel growled, he bared his teeth. The puppy didn't move again. Axel went around the enclosure and picked up the three treats one at a time and put them into a container.

The lid closed. He repeated until he had the yard cleared. He yipped at the puppy and it ran to him. He licked it. We knew this worked with Digger and Sally, but Chili had a stubborn streak.

CHAPTER 27

Roger called. "How's the case going?"

"Good and bad," I answered. "We know the connection between the people who were murdered. They were all on a jury over thirty-years ago. A serial killer by the name of John Michael Malloy was the defendant. Does it sound familiar?"

"Barely. I was still in the academy. I only know what a sensation it was. Twelve jurors, with more than enough proof to convict a serial killer, let him go. The judge did nothing and Malloy was killed a week or two later while trying to catch a train at Union Station."

"Not only did they beat him to death, but he had six bullet holes in him. It has always been a mystery why they acquitted him. We all know they were paid off, but no one could track down who paid the money. Not one of those people talked. After a few years, they all became successful, the publicity settled down and it was no longer news."

"I wonder why all these years later someone is killing them? It doesn't take a genius to figure out whoever set it up in the first place is the killer."

I had put Roger on speaker the minute he began to talk. When I answered, everyone was up to snuff on the conversation. "The way we figure it, someone has either decided to clear their conscience before they die, or one of them might be blackmailing the blackmailer. It would be easier to track all of this if it wasn't such a cold case. We will figure it out."

"I wanted to check in. I know I have been no help during this investigation. Between Covid, the flu and people having to stay home because of sick children, all I am is a glorified babysitter trying to cover shifts.

"One reason I took this job was so I could be out on the street. I don't mean to bitch, but this is really getting old. Keep in touch. If I can do anything for you, let me know."

"As a matter of fact," I said, "you can. Send someone to the archives and have the transcript of the trial sent to us."

"It might not have been transferred to digital yet. You might have to read it in the archives. I'll let you know." He hung up.

Ryan looked at his phone. "Time flies when you're having fun. Nathan and I need to go to the office. I have a meeting with Samuel Trucking about putting new GPS in their trucks. Nathan has a meeting with Jones Trash Haulers.

"People keep sneaking into the land fill looking for treasures. We need to light up the entire fence to keep people out. That place isn't stable. Someone's going to get buried in the rubble."

CHAPTER 28

Ryan didn't make it home until after eight. Amy and I had found the addresses of the remainder of the jurors. Three had died since the trial. We had four to visit and warn. Seems alternates were not a big thing all those years ago.

People were called to jury duty and they went. They didn't call in another person unless absolutely necessary. We decided to go about eleven in the morning.

Amy had laundry to finish and even though we had a housekeeper, we kept the office and all the equipment locked up. I liked to clean it myself once a week and get rid of all of the useless information from old cases. There could be hundreds of pages of notes no one would ever look at again.

Amy showed up at eleven as expected. She didn't have the dogs with her. "What's up? Where are Sally and Digger?"

"We aren't sure what's going on. The outside alarms went off four times last night. Nathan and Sally went out to check. Someone wanted to get in. They broke out three planks from the fence near the garden.

"Nathan dusted for fingerprints. Nothing. We decided to leave Sally home to protect the homestead. Digger wanted to stay with her. We talked it over and decided he was safe with Sally."

I tried to take her mind off the break-in. "How much longer will you have veggies. Isn't the weather getting too cold?

"The first hard freeze is next Wednesday. Nathan and I actually bought a deep freezer and a vacuum sealer. He is taking half a day off to pick today and tonight and the weekend we will package it all.

Amy laughed. "I never thought it would happen, but we are regular little farmers."

"Tell me about the alarms. What time did they go off?"

"It was nearly midnight the first time and the other two were an hour apart. I believe someone thought we would chalk it up to the wind. Usually when these things happen it is because of a case you and I are working on. This time I think we were going to get robbed."

No sooner then she had got the words out of her mouth, the phones went off. Dispatch had an announcement.

Amy answered her phone, turned on the speaker and sat it on the table. The messages were nearly always cryptic.

"Homicide, Arlene Noble, white female, age 74, 1463 Milky Way Dr. Neighbor called 911. Locals are on the way."

I looked at Amy. "She is on the list of people we

were going to talk to today. I feel as if it is my fault."

Amy put her hand on my shoulder. "I realize we should have talked to her sooner, but we don't know it would have saved her."

I let the dogs outside and when they came in I locked the pet door behind them and left them loose to roam the house. In my heart I knew two things: Axel would never hurt Chili, and he would never let anyone in the house.

Even though I knew Amy and Nathan's problems at their house last night had nothing to do with us, I couldn't be too careful.

Milky Way Drive ran parallel to Chambers Road. Each of the six houses were on a cul-de-sac with an electric gate so the dwellers could get onto the street. It was no more than a gated community with six houses in every little community.

The homes were huge, brick structures with giant brick and concrete porches and expensive landscaping. The Nobles lived in the fourth house on the left. It turned out Arlene Noble had survived everyone in the family and had been paying handsomely for home care.

She and Naomie Hurst, her niece and caretaker, had returned from the grocery store ten minutes before what her niece referred to as the accident happened. As Naomie pulled into their driveway, she heard a pop. She attributed it to a blowout until she noticed her aunt lay slumped against the passenger side door with a neat little hole in her head and one to match in the car windshield.

Thank goodness no one had touched a thing. Mrs. Hurst still lay with her head against the window and half of her brains spread all over the front seat and her niece.

Naomie Hurst didn't see a thing. No one walked alone on the streets during the day. Most were elderly and waited for family before they went out. The gate stayed locked unless one of the inhabitants rolled down their window and put in a four-digit code.

I wondered why anyone who could afford to live in these million dollar plus houses didn't have a digital code they could enter with a phone or a garage opener styled device,

Amy must have been thinking along the same lines because she asked, "Why isn't the gate set up so you don't have to roll down the window to open it?"

The niece answered. "All of the owners are the same age or older than Aunt Arlene. It is difficult to get them to try anything new."

"Who would want your aunt dead?" I asked.

"No one I know of. She rarely leaves the house. We grocery shop on Wednesday afternoon and her bridge club meets every other Thursday night in the back room at the Spaghetti House."

"Did your aunt ever tell you about a sensational trial of a serial killer? She sat on the jury." I guided her toward the back door.

"No. I do know an event happened about thirty years ago. She'd never tell any of us what happened. People said she rarely went anywhere after the incident happened. It has only been four or five years since she began joining me to get groceries, and last year, she began to go to a bridge club."

Amy asked, "Did your mother say anything that might give you a clue as to what happened all those years ago?"

"No, none. I only know she thought she saw someone who followed her all of the time. She was afraid he would kill her. She never gave a serious reason for it, so I chalked it up to old age and a little paranoia."

Once we guided her into the kitchen and all sat at a huge round oak table with ornate chairs, I said, "Would you be surprised to know your aunt sat on the jury when a notorious serial killer was tried for murder and the jury acquitted him?"

She put both hands up to her mouth. "Seems a little far-fetched to me. When did it happen?"

"Around thirty years ago. What did your aunt do for a living which afforded her this huge house and beautiful expensive furniture?"

She moved her hands a little bit away from her mouth. "She taught English at a local school in Clayton. It has nothing to do with the house. It and all the others on these two streets," she waved her hand to encompass everything in a large area, "were built in the late 1800's. To the best of my knowledge they have been handed down generation to generation. I don't believe any of them have ever been sold outside the family.

"I saw the deed once, when my uncle died. The house was built in 1865. The total cost was in the high hundreds. They are the fifth generation to live here. When Auntie is gone, it will be mine."

"Will you sell it?" I asked.

"No, never. I always tried not to think about it for fear someone would think I wanted my aunt out of the way. There is a house on the other side of Forest Park. Are you familiar with it?"

Amy opened her mouth to speak and I cut her off.

"No, is it a house like this?"

"I went over once when the Meade boy turned it into a museum and public park. I'd love to do it here. I only need a few rooms. The house has eight bedrooms, seven and a half bathrooms, two kitchens, a pantry and food prep room as large as another kitchen. I could go on and on. I doubt I'll ever get it done unless all the old ones die and the new ones all agree it's the way to go."

Amy got up and took a closer look at the table, the gorgeous knick-knacks and ornate hutches in the house. "Miss Hurst, it is Miss, right?"

"Yes, yes, it is."

"How did Mrs. Noble afford the upkeep on the place?"

"I'm not sure. I assumed she inherited. I know all six of the streets and the houses on each street has a special zoning. The taxes are no more than a modest home. It is on the National Registry. She kept most of her history to herself."

"But you never talked about her life?"

"No, no we didn't. Wait, Aunt Arlene wrote in a journal. She wrote every night after we said goodnight. I could hear her up. I'm sure there are volumes and volumes. I've lived here fifteen years and she has always written."

I stood. "Where are those books?" I asked.

"I'm not sure I should. They were personal. I didn't even read them."

"Miss Hurst," I said, "this is a crime scene. We can get a search warrant, but it seems as if it would be a big waste of time."

"You can have them so far as I'm concerned. I would like to have them back when you are done with them."

Amy and Naomie went off toward the staircase, and I went back outside to the body and the investigation.

The teams swarmed around like bees in the spring. The body had been moved into an ambulance. The car sat on a trailer to be taken to the auto crime lab. I stopped Raymond Stoop, the lead CSI. "What do you think?"

"There is not much here. No sign of anyone near the car. No fingerprints on the fence where the bullet had to come from. No foot prints. No stippling on the skin, meaning the kill shot wasn't close up." He pointed to a spot where a grouping of dwarf maples grew near the sidewalk two blocks away. "I know it was a long rifle and I believe a 2-43 or a 30 ought 6 . It could be as simple as someone wanted to kill someone today and she drew the short straw."

I filled him in on the other murders all being from a jury thirty years ago. He shook his head. "Once the M.E. gets the body and the car makes it to the forensic garage, we'll call you. This is a terrible neighborhood for shootings.

"Developers try to buy the rest of these gated houses to turn them into apartments. There is some kind of association. One won't sell unless they all do."

Amy came out of the house with a leather satchel over her shoulder. "These are the journals. Guess we'd better check them in at the Evidence Room before we take them home. We don't want to lose a case because we didn't have an evidence chain. I'll get an evidence card from one of the guys and meet you at the car."

I patted the briefcase Amy set on the console

between us. "As much as I want to read those, let's drop in on Andrew Simpson and Roger Farr while they are still breathing."

"Agreed. Donnetta Reginald died of cancer in 1996, Margaret Hines-Chase died of natural causes. She was the oldest, in her sixties back then. Deon Jeffreys was shot by police during a robbery gone wrong."

"Strange bedfellows."

We headed the opposite direction to try to find a gentleman named Andrew Simpson. "Andrew lives in a senior assisted living apartment near Mars and General," Amy said.

"I know exactly where it is. Remember when the old lady thought aliens were trying to get her? The place is directly across the street."

Amy turned in her seat to face me more directly. "Do you know what I hate most about this police job?" She didn't give me time to answer. "We have had absolutely no fun. I want our cases back, like the guy who wanted to kill his neighbor's cat."

I laughed. "And the husband who thought his wife was having an affair but the women's club had moved to a motel because the minister eavesdropped on them?"

"No more cases for the police. I don't know how I did it before, but I never want to do it again," Amy said.

I slapped her hand in a high five. "Copy that."

The apartment building looked the same. I had a pang of sadness knowing the old lady no longer lived there. The senior living center across the street looked new, although we knew it wasn't. The bushes were trimmed for the coming winter. Roses were mulched and the sidewalks didn't have a leaf on them.

Before we got out of the car, Amy put her hand on my forearm. "How do you want to handle this?" she asked.

"Let's hit it head on, come right out and ask him why they acquitted a serial killer. Where did the money come from and who was behind it?"

"Do you think we will learn anymore?" she asked.

"Well, we can't know less than we do now. I don't see where we have anything to lose."

I pulled into one of the parking spots directly in front of the door marked Visitor Parking.

The inside shined like the outside. The floors were spotless, no handprints on the walls, no chip marks where a wheelchair might have dinged it, and a pretty lady in her late sixties behind a desk who greeted us with a friendly smile. "May I help you?"

"Yes," I said. "We'd like to visit with Andrew Simson."

"Let me check the book and see where he is at the moment." She pulled out a schedule book and began to flip through it. Here it is.

"He is in the sitting room reading. It is the third door down. Andrew will be the man in the silk pajamas and robe sitting in front of the window at the left end of the room. Most likely he will be the only one with a book in his hand. "Most of our residents prefer the TV or a board game."

As we walked toward the sitting room Amy whispered, "It sounded like she wanted to show us a room for ourselves rather than tell us where the man was."

I grinned at her.

Andrew Simpson sat ramrod straight in an

upholstered chair right were the receptionist said he would be. If I had to describe him to anyone, I would have used the word regal. He had a full head of silver hair and a thin mustache just above his upper lip yet not thick enough to notice from across the room. He had a book in his hand.

He didn't look up. He either didn't want to talk to us or didn't realize we were there. I reached into my back pocket and took out a card and put it in the fold of the book he appeared to be reading.

He looked up, picked up the card and read it aloud. "Nash and Perkin Detective Agency. Ladies, I believe you have the wrong person. I didn't call for a detective."

I opened my jacket so he could see my St. Louis Police badge. Without being asked, Amy and I pulled chairs up on each side of him and prepared to have a conversation with the man.

He looked first at Amy then turned his head toward me. "Which is it, are you a cop or a private detective?"

I answered him. "We are private but working a case for the St. Louis Police department because they had too many people out sick. I was a cop there a few years ago. Amy was a cop in Chicago."

"If you want to talk to me, you will have to put your chairs closer together in front of me. I don't want to engage in a ping-pong game instead of a conversation." He smiled a straight white toothed smile.

"What kind of work did you do before you retired, Mr. Simpson?"

"I actually didn't work. Well, I did, but never away from my studio. I'm an artist."

Amy leaned forward to make sure she had his

attention. "Sorry, I don't mean to hurt your feelings. My knowledge of artists is nonexistent."

He gave Amy one of his award winning smiles. "My feelings are not hurt. I spent my life doing what I loved to do. It's the path to happiness. Now what do homicide detectives want with me. I swear I've managed to make it to age ninety-two and I've managed not to kill a single soul."

"We want to talk to you about a murder trial. It happened over thirty-years ago."

He sat up a little straighter. "The serial killer? Yes, I was not a part of any other trial."

"I read the transcript," I said. "Seems like the man was undoubtedly guilty."

"Yes, he was."

"Why did you vote to acquit him?"

He closed the book he held and put it on a table beside him. "I have never talked to a soul about what happened. We were each offered twenty-five thousand dollars to vote not guilty. It was a life changing amount of money back then. I thought about it for days. Then I said, yes, once the man said the killer would still be put to death, just not by the state."

I couldn't read Amy's look when she glanced my way. "Why are you telling us this?"

"Because he has killed most of the people who sat on that jury. It is only a matter of time before he comes after me. I'm ninety-two, have a bad heart, no loved ones left on this plane. I'd rather go out my way than sit around here wondering when he is going to come after me."

"Mr. Simpson, tell us who it is and we will stop him."

"I don't know who he is."

"How do you know who the other people on the jury are? They do everything to keep you away from the public?" Amy said.

"But no one policed our conversations. You're not even allowed to talk to the others except to discuss the case." Simpson said. His face went pale and he put his hand on his chest. "Please have someone get my pills out of my room, and quickly."

Someone was watching us because a woman appeared at his side with a pill he put under his tongue. The nurse looked up from tending to him and said, "He always leaves his nitro in his room. I keep an extra bottle in my pocket." She looked down at the man. "If you are tired or in distress, I can have these ladies come back."

"No, no. I want to talk to them."

We sat quietly until he spoke again. Hopefully he could put a period at the end of this case.

He looked from one of us to the other. "Sorry ladies. I spend most of my time with a book or quiet music. I know my heart won't last much longer. I'd like to clear this up."

Amy put her hand on the arm of his chair. He smiled at us.

"I will do my best to explain what happened in the courtroom but more importantly what happened in the jury room.

"The judge told us the defense would finish their presentation in one more day. It was the last day we could talk to our families. We were allowed to say hi to our children and husbands or wives and that was all.

"We were sequestered for the duration of the

deliberations. The newspapers went wild. They were sure it would only be a few hours before we came back with a guilty plea. Before we all agreed, two weeks had passed.

"And it wasn't a verdict we agreed on. What we agreed on was a bribe. An anonymous person offered each of us on the jury money to acquit the man. None of us had an inkling who it was. Some folks had parents to take care of, others had sick kids, mortgages they couldn't pay. You know, life."

I leaned forward and looked him right in the eye. It all sounded far-fetched to me. "How on earth would someone be able to bribe an entire jury?"

"Remember this happened in 1992. We had computers but not like today. Actually the first text was sent in 1992. Everyone read the newspaper back then. Of course we were not allowed to read or hear any news at all.

"We would go to the jury room in the morning and breakfast would already be there. Same with lunch. We came in, the food was there for us, dinner the same way. We were allowed to go to a brick enclosed patio in the back of the building. On top of the wall razor wire ran from end to end.

"On our second day of deliberation, a woman by the name of Margaret Hines-Chase, took a bite of a fish sandwich and a paper fell out. It was a rather cryptic message:' Enough is enough, the killing must stop, his and yours. Innocent is how you should vote. I'll tell you why in another note.'"

I stood and stretched my back. "How long did this go on?"

"Over a week. At first we thought it to be a joke.

Then we decided someone wanted to catch us with the notes and call a mistrial. The second week the judge called us in several times and asked if we thought we could ever agree to a verdict."

"We told him yes but by now there was proof the person behind the letters was not joking. A man on the jury, Victor Mann, had received a letter under his door in the hotel. It had a bank account number with a deposit slip for the money. The next night, three more people received them."

"I've been a banker all my life. For years I ran the Third National Bank of Missouri. I knew the deposit slips were real. They were made into small banks in the East and North East."

"Just when I thought it to be a joke or a crazy man, the pool began to talk seriously of acquitting the man. Instead of deliberating, we spent all of our time talking about what the worst things that could happen to us were."

"We all knew if we took the money, we were putting ourselves up for a constant threat of blackmail. Some of us just didn't want to let the monster go. This went on for days.

"On the sixteenth day of deliberations we sent word we had a verdict. We let him go."

Amy leaned forward and nearly whispered her question, "Did the judge ask for a mistrial?"

"No, we'd been around the people of the court long enough to believe they bribed the judge also."

"We swore we would never tell anything that happened in that room and until now, I think it has been true. Well, I did until I began seeing the stories of the deaths of the jurors. I decided eventually whoever it is will get to me."

"I don't want to take the world's greatest con to the grave with me." He let out a deep breath and his entire body relaxed and his eyes closed.

I believed he had passed. I reached toward his neck and was about to feel for a pulse when he said, "I'm okay. This is the lightest I have felt in thirty years."

I asked, "Why do you think after all these years, the person behind this is beginning to kill the witnesses?"

"My honest opinion is that one of the victims is related to the person who set this all up. Something has changed in his life to make him want everyone who had anything to do with it dead. The judge retired but mysteriously fell while hiking in the Grand Canyon. He was the first to go. That was about ten years ago."

"One more thing," Amy asked, "why do you think he went to all the trouble and spent all that money when Malloy would get the death penalty anyway?"

"None of us knew why until three weeks later when Malloy left to board a train at three in the morning. Someone emptied a shotgun into his belly. After that we thought we knew the revenge the person wanted was worth over a million dollars to him.

"I think it was so he could have the pleasure of killing the guy himself instead of taking a chance he would sit on death row for years. Of course, that's just my opinion.

"For the first year, I watched carefully when I went out and made sure I didn't run into anyone from the jury. After a while it is like everything else. You get used to it, a cast, a missing foot, bad eyesight. Our body and minds adjust to all of it."

Amy leaned forward. "Do you think someone, or

more than one person, had been blackmailing him all this time and decided, enough was enough? Maybe he didn't know who it was so he set out to kill all of you?"

"I doubt it. Could be a guilty conscience or remorse. One of us did something to trigger this. Only the killer knows. One thing has stuck with me since the trial. They questioned every mother, father, sister, roommate, spouse, jeez, everyone they could think of, who was related to or had any interaction with the victims. One man used the phrase, enough is enough, when they kept hammering him about the details around his relative's death. They had him on the stand for nearly three days. I have never been able to remember his name. The more time has passed, the more I remember him using the phrase.

"It stuck out because whoever put the money in our bank accounts used the phrase to persuade us to go alone with the scheme.

"Can you describe him?" I asked.

"Heavens no, I can barely remember what my beloved wife looked like. My two greatest sins were to agree to let a killer walk free and to not come forward when I had this all fresh in my memory."

We could tell he had taxed himself. He rubbed his chest, put a hand gently on one of each of our knees. "You will never know how sorry I am about this. I could sit here and tell you a million excuses why I did it. But the truth is, I was greedy."

We said our goodbyes and somehow, I was sad for the man. I know wrongs don't turn into rights, but I breathed a little prayer for him. Maybe I am a softy.

CHAPTER 29

We had one more juror to see, Andrew Simmons, an entertainer who lived in Branson. We decided to ask the police down in the Country Western Capital of the World to look in on him for us.

"Hi, this is Detective Kate Nash, St. Louis Homicide."

"This is Thomas McCoy, I'm the deputy who keeps it all together down here, or at least I try. What can I do for you?"

"I'm sure, unless you live under a rock, you know we have a serial killer in our midst. We have one more person who we think is on his list to kill."

"We are familiar," he said. "Don't tell me he is coming our way."

I tried to chuckle. "No, but you have a man down there who we think might be his next victim."

The tone of his voice changed, and I could tell he took my call seriously. "A man by the name of Andrew Simmons."

It turned silent and I thought he hung up, "Sergeant McCoy, are you there?"

"Yes, I am. I do think it is strange we found Mr. Simmons floating in knee deep water in Lake Taneycomo three days ago. We have not been able to find any next of kin. For the last two days I've had my people in his home. We haven't found anything.

"Had you not called we would have thought he drowned. Now I don't know what to think."

I always put my cell phone on speaker when Amy was within hearing distance. I looked at her. She shrugged. "How did he die?"

"According to the other fishermen around him, he tried to jump out of his boat by the shore instead of a dock. He ended up knee deep in mud. Several people tried to help him, but he stood six-feet-four and weighed a good two hundred and eighty-pounds. He passed out and they couldn't keep his head above water until more help came. I can tell you they tried.

"He would have died anyway. Later we discovered he had a bullet in his back."

"One more question."

"Sure."

"Why do you think he jumped out of the boat instead of stepping over the side?"

"Everyone would like to know why. Personally, the chief and I think he tried to get some cover from the shooter, but he'd been hit and couldn't help himself out of the boat the way he needed to."

"Thanks for your help."

"You are more than welcome. If you need anything else, let me know. I will tell you he was pretty much a recluse and a minimalist. There sure wasn't much in his house."

"Thanks again, McCoy. I'll call again if we think of anything else important to the case."

"Why do you think he was killed by your killer?"

"We have a list. I'm not at liberty to disclose where we obtained the list at this time. What I can tell you is Mr. Simmons was the last person on that list. He's killed most of the people on the list. We know why he did it. So Malloy wouldn't get appeals, stays of execution, new trials and all of that. We know how he did it. What we don't know is who he is."

After I hung up, Amy asked, "Why didn't you ask about ENUFSENUF?"

"I thought of it just as we were hanging up. I have the number. I'll text and ask him."

Ten minutes later a picture showed up on my phone from McCoy's number. The picture showed a business card like all the rest we had seen. No doubt who killed him.

I asked Amy, "Do you think we should go through the personnel records from the courts?"

She looked my way and shook her head no. "We'd have to cross out anyone over sixty-four. Those jobs have mandatory retirement. Any combination adding to thirty-years on the job and you are out. I think the answer lies with a relative of one of the victims."

Not only was I frustrated, but the entire situation caused my body to involuntarily shudder. "This is the last warm day for nearly two weeks. Want to take the dogs for a walk?"

"Sure, "she said. "So long as we don't go to Ted Drew's."

"Let's walk to my house, get Digger and Sally, walk

around the park and have Ryan pick you up on his way home."

"Sounds wonderful. I'll leave him a message and see if it fits into his schedule."

We went to the kitchen and picked up four water bottles. One for each of us and one each for the dogs. We only walked about fifteen steps when the breeze turned from the South to the North. "I'll go back and grab us a jacket. Be right back," I said.

When I came back, someone was shooting. Chili barked and ran into the house. Amy crouched down between the bushes, not much cover if she needed it. Axel ran at me and nearly knocked me down. Until then, I hadn't heard a shot.

We'd lived on a cul-de-sac off of Brentwood Boulevard. We were used to the traffic and the noise of the cars and trucks. A first shot must have put Axel on guard and caused Chili to run into the house.

Another shot rang out and hit a window in our office. "Axel," Amy said in a soft voice, "I know you are a guard dog but you can't go up against a long rifle. Whoever it is would shoot you before you got close enough to disarm him."

"It's coming from behind the repair truck over there on the next block. We need to get inside," I said.

I already heard sirens. No one could shoot a gun in this neighborhood without someone calling it in.

Axel crawled on his belly to the far side of the house where a bullet couldn't reach. He barked softly for Amy and me to follow. I took my 9 mm Glock out of the waistband of my jeans and began to fire in the direction of the shooter.

I'm not sure why. I knew I couldn't reach him. A

long distance rifle had me out gunned and out distanced.

I tried to follow my shot as best I could. Last thing I wanted was to accidentally kill a neighbor. Once we turned the corner and had a brick wall between her and the shooter, Amy pulled her Ruger and covered me.

The police cruiser came directly to the house. The next time we had a chance to look that way, the shooter was no longer around.

CHAPTER 30

Ryan skidded up to the sidewalk, barely missing a police cruiser. Nathan jumped out of the passenger seat while Ryan came from the other side of his truck without closing the door.

"How did you get here so soon?" Amy asked Nathan.

"Instead of Jacob being the only one who can hear the scanner, he has it passing through every speaker in the office. We got the call the instant the police did."

Ryan already had me in his arms. He pushed me away from him far enough to see my face. "What happened?"

I took another step back. "We found the last juror who was killed three days ago in Branson. He was shot in the back, went into the lake and drown. The ever present business card was found at his home.

"The entire situation hit me worse than usual and we decided to go for a walk. We didn't get ten steps before the shooting started. Had I not gone back to get Amy and me a jacket, we would have had no cover what-so-ever."

"We may have gotten a break, though," Amy said. "A bullet went through the window on the side of the door. I imagine the spent shell shouldn't be hard to find."

One of the officers stood next to us while we talked. He took notes and called a CSI team and before it arrived, Roger Simon arrived.

We all went inside and sat in the living room.

Ryan didn't bother to ask any of us if we wanted a drink. He handed Amy and me a glass of Merlot, and Roger, Nathan and himself a beer.

No one said a word. CSI personnel were all over the front door and hallway. The shell had gone through the window, went down the hall, hit a kitchen cabinet and ended up in a tree in the backyard.

The thought I couldn't get out of my head amounted to the fact that if an AR15 shell had hit one of us in the hand, it would have blown an entire arm off. The next thing on my mind, the one that bothered me the most, was why did the killer upgrade his gun to a complete automatic military rifle?

Because he wanted to kill us. I knew it.

Ryan was knelt in front of me with his hand on my knee. "Kate, did you hear what I said?"

I looked up, but I couldn't quite get my brain to engage. No one had ever wanted to kill me so badly they were prepared to blow me into little pieces. Was it because we were closer to the answer?

"Kate," Amy said, in a louder voice than Ryan used. "Are you okay?"

I looked from Amy to Ryan to Roger to Nathan. "Why are you all staring at me?"

"Because you left us for a moment or two," Roger said.

"Sorry. I am confused, I guess. Why try to kill us? We are no closer to knowing who killed those twelve people than we were the day we started this investigation," I said.

Ryan stood and began to walk back and forth across the living room. "Apparently the killer doesn't know that. I believe we should take some time tomorrow and go over everything we know about these murders. We might have the answer to who the killer is and not realize it."

"Why not now," I asked.

Amy stood and walked over to the wine bottle on the end table. "We aren't up to it; you're not the only one shocked about the turn of events."

Roger held his empty bottle up. Ryan took it and walked toward the kitchen to get him another. "Before you call it a night, can someone fill me in on the latest?"

Amy took over. "We found out the last juror killed lived in Branson. They found the Enuf is Enuf card in his home. I believe the same person who killed the jurors didn't bribe them in the first place. I think the first man wanted to make sure Malloy never had a chance to appeal."

"So why kill all of those other people?" Roger asked.

"It's personal, right?" Ryan asked me.

"I believe so." I answered and emptied the wine glass I'd been holding. I got up, looked at everyone in the room and said, "I'm going to bed."

CHAPTER 31

I hated busy work. Whenever I had to stop and go over old material, I found it a waste of time. On the bright side, he couldn't kill us if we were inside the house and not sticking our heads out to take a chance of getting a shot off.

Amy and I were in the office with the four dogs, black coffee (unheard for us), and cinnamon rolls. Instead of getting on with the task at hand, I stared at the wall in front of me.

The office had been Ryan's, the security pros at his office, and Jacob his computer guru's project. My only input was the color of the room. I wanted yellow. Yellow happened to be my favorite color. Not baseball uniform yellow, more like butter yellow.

Amy and I went to the Benjamin Moore store where the paint expert convinced us to put lime green in with the yellow to brighten it up. Since then, I sometimes got lost in a crusade to find the lime. I never could. As a bonus, yellow inspired creativity.

Well, for fifteen minutes I'd been looking at it and I

didn't feel more creative than when I came in. Both of the dogs must have sensed something wrong. Chili sat at my feet begging to be held and Axel moved out of his bed to lay next to me.

Amy cleared her throat and said, "You need to get over this blue funk you're in. It isn't getting anywhere but to make me extremely nervous. Snap out of it. The faster we figure this out, the sooner we can get away for a few days.

"I'm thinking we need some beach time. Maybe the Keys."

I reached down and picked up Chili. "I can't put it together. First he goes to great lengths to dress up like a woman, get someone to drive him around in a white limo, then he ditches the scenario, sinks the car in the Mississippi River, burns the truck he used to hide it and begins to murder willy-nilly; shoot or stab, he doesn't care.

"If he is the one who bribed the jurors to let Malloy free so he could have the joy of killing the killer himself, why wait over thirty years to do it?"

While I talked, she turned on the computers, scanners and the other equipment. Before she had a chance to say anything, my phone rang. Caller ID read Roger Simon. I pressed answer, then speaker and laid it on my desk. "What's up Roger?"

"Oh, just another mystery. My guys found the AR15 leaning against a tree two blocks over outside of a vacant garage."

"Any idea who it belongs to?"

"Sort of. It once belonged to a Tymon Bell who registered it some twenty years ago. He might still own it, but after all these years, it could be in anybody's hands. I'll text you his last known address. Maybe you should pay him a visit."

"Good idea. We are on our way. We'll let you know what happens."

I pushed the disconnect call button and looked up toward Amy, who had stood and leaned against my desk. Amy had been my best friend for a few years before I opened Kate Nash Investigations. Business took off, Amy took on more and more responsibility and before long the business became Nash and Perkin Investigations.

As I look up at her now, once again, her look always amazed me, maybe I was secretly jealous. She wore an emerald green silk blouse with an open collar, a tiny diamond pendant, and tailored black slacks. As always, she wore a pair of cheaters around her neck, this time on a green and black ribbon.

"Let's go talk to this guy. He has to know what he did with the gun."

She pushed herself to an upright position and went to her computer. "Tymon Bell, age 69, Army Major, retired. Widower, two male children, Tymon Jr. age 50 and Jamal, age 52, both married with children. They own an auto body shop. No arrests, parking tickets, or blemishes on his record. Last known address: 2777 Marshall Rd. St. Louis. Should we take the dogs?"

I stood, picked up my Glock from a shelf near the door and called the dogs to go outside before we left. I didn't need to take them, but no way could Axel and Sally protect the babies or themselves from bullets.

The house sat on a cul-du-sac at the end of a beautifully landscaped row of homes on what looked to be three to five acres. A light-skinned black man had a leaf blower, most likely cleaning up for winter. He stopped when we pulled into his driveway and walked toward the car.

Nobody had to tell me he had a military background. He stood about six-feet-two, squared shoulder and the physique and manner of a much younger man.

He walked over to the car and I rolled down the window. "What can I do for you ladies today?"

I took my badge out of my pocket. "I'm Detective Kate Nash, this is my partner, Detective Amy Perkin. We would like to ask you a few questions about a gun registered to you."

He took two steps back. "Sure, come on out of the car and we can sit on the porch." He looked toward the graying sky. "This weather isn't going to hold. Won't be long before we will have to spend more of the time inside."

Major Bell opened my door. Amy got out from her side and came around. "You have a beautiful home," she said.

"Thanks. My wife's pride and joy. She died seven years ago. I know you'll think I'm crazy, but I chat with Missy while I weed her flowers and seed her lawn."

"I think it is sweet," I said.

He led us to an immaculate front porch with the last blooms of a purple clematis climbing up a latice used to hide a table and four chairs from the street. "Can I get you ladies something to drink."

"No thanks, Major Bell. We don't want to take up too much of your time," I said.

He looked from me to Amy and back. "This sounds serious. I guess you'd better tell me what it is about."

Amy nodded at me to speak. "Yesterday, an AK15

was found leaning against a tree in U City. It's registered to you. Do you know how it got under that tree?"

"I wish I could," he said. "We had a robbery here about twelve years ago and it got taken along with three other long guns, four pistols and a huge amount of ammunition. My youngest son was here at the time. The thieves beat him so badly he spent over a week in intensive care. He still has a limp."

While he talked, Amy had taken out her notebook and began jotting down facts. "Was there a police report?"

"Oh, yes, and a trial. The men were caught. So far as I know they're still locked up. The guns went into the police evidence room all those years ago. They are either still there or, actually, I figured they were destroyed after all of this time."

I believed every word he said. "Thanks for the information. There are twelve thousand people who could have taken those guns over the years."

"What do you mean twelve thousand people."

Amy said, "She is counting all of the folks who have worked in the police department, court system and could have had access to the guns."

Major Bell walked us to the car. He opened the door for me, and I said, "I think those we love who have gone before us, know the chores and love we put out in remembrance of them. I bet your wife smiles on you daily."

I had my hand on the window sill, he put his on mine. "Thank you for that. My youngest hates to come here because of what happened to him. My other has young children and not much time. Knowing Missy is still able to appreciate what I do around here makes all of the work worthwhile. You ladies be careful out there."

"What do you think?" I asked Amy as we drove back to the heart of the city.

"He's telling the truth. Everything he told us is easily verified. I say he really has no idea how the gun ended up where it did."

CHAPTER 32

With some investigations, we learned, thirty years ago, you needed a key to get into the evidence room and a book to sign in. No one sat at the door as they did now to make sure the person who signed it out was the same as his ID.

A semi-retired officer, who now ran the desk at the Thirteenth Precinct, a guy named Max Malone, told us there could have been hundreds of keys copied so the people who needed the information could come and go as they pleased.

"Remember," he said, "we didn't have the drug problem we have now. Cases were about a tenth of what they are now. Nobody, well only a few, sat in jail for months or years waiting for their case to come up.

"Police most usually made their case before they arrested the perp. It was more like Law and Order back then. Mostly the evidence only went to court and came back. And more people looked at it. The police, lawyers, prosecutors, the medical examiner, and sometimes they sent people who were just runners to pick up and return the items."

Amy and I looked at one another. "One more question," I said. "Can we find out if all the guns from a case thirty years ago are gone. We found one was used in an attempted murder yesterday."

"Without even looking I can say with certainty, no guns over twenty years old are gone. They were destroyed. It was a pet project of the mayor back then."

"Thanks for your help, sir."

He gave us a quick salute, more a friendly gesture than a sign of reverence.

"What now?" I asked Amy.

"Let's grab some lunch to take with us and head back to the office. I still believe with all my heart, it is a relative of one of the victims."

"It's better than anything I have right now. Where do you want to get lunch?"

"Subway. I love their veggie sandwiches. I feel like I'm eating healthy but I still get bread."

Twenty minutes later we were in the office, sandwiches spread on the desks and a list of the serial killer's victims.

We wolfed down the sandwiches and refilled our drinks before we settled down to tackle the list. Of course, we'd been gone for hours and the dogs wanted to play. We looked at one another and wordlessly we agreed to go outside with them.

Late afternoon caught up with us before we settled down in earnest. The work was tedious. There were eleven victims John Michael Malloy confessed to and another six Dr. Dane Willis, who had started as Medical Examiner only six months before the first killing, swore were killed in exactly the same way as the original eleven.

The history of the crimes Dane Willis gave us at the beginning of our investigation couldn't have been more thorough. At nearly six-thirty, I heard Ryan come in through the garage, as did the dogs.

I stood, and let them out of the office to go meet him. We followed them out. "How's it going," he said when he saw us.

Amy and I said at almost the same time, "Every clue is another dead end or blind corner."

Ryan walked over and kissed me. "I think you two have worked together too long. You're like an old married couple finishing one another's sentences."

How true it was.

"My idea, which I haven't shared with Amy yet, is that we go down and visit with Dr. Willis. He seemed to be obsessed with the entire ordeal and wrote a complete history of the entire case."

"The entire killing run took place over a four-year span. Instead of spending any more long hours on the tiny details, I think we need to question Willis."

At the same time Amy and Ryan both said, "Good idea."

I couldn't help but say to Ryan," Does that mean you and Amy are like an old married couple.?"

Amy pulled a chair out from the dining room table and perched on the edge of it. "Where is Nathan? I've tried to reach him twice today. It isn't like him not to call back."

"He should be at home by now. I would guess he headed straight to the shower," Ryan said.

"Is he okay," Amy asked.

"Yes, just uncomfortable. He just finished a final

walk-through at the Quick Lube offices and was on his way to his truck when he got a call from one of the branches wanting him to come back. They said the alarm system in their building would not connect with the rest of the system or the office.

"He drove back. Seems a five-year old, who came with his father to get the oil changed in their car, threw the remote control of the system into a can of old oil before the men closing up had a chance to put a lid on it.

"The kid heard them talking about what the problem was. At the same time, he reached back into the oil can and retrieved the missing part. He threw it to Nathan. Oil went in Nathan's hair, on his clothes and shoes, but mostly his face and hands.

"He drove his truck home. One of the guys from the oil company followed him and took his truck to have it detailed. Let's just say, Nathan just wanted a shower, a beer and a quiet evening."

"Oh, my," Amy said. "I'd better head home. I think I'll go by the Spaghetti Shack and pick up dinner on my way home. See you guys tomorrow."

Without Digger, Sally and Amy in the house, it seemed especially quiet.

CHAPTER 33

"**D**o you realize how long it has been since we spent any time together?" Ryan asked.

I got off the couch and walked over to where he stood next to the sliding door. "We could change that," I said, reaching for him.

We moved to the couch and were making out and joking with one another when Ryan suggested we make dinner and go to bed early.

I stood, "What are you hungry for?"

"That's a loaded question I don't intend to answer."

"How about a grilled cheese sandwich and tomato basil soup?"

He already stood near the refrigerator. "Sounds wonderful. You get the soup ready and I'll grill the cheese."

On my way to the pantry he asked, "Is rye good?"

"Always."

Twenty minutes later we were at the dining room table with a Pepsi, grilled American on Rye and Doritos. We rarely ate junk food dinners. I found it especially tasty on this night. We took the dogs for a walk together and ran into every neighbor we knew. Of course, everyone wanted to question us about what happened earlier.

These are the same neighbors who saw us taken down, handcuffed and taken away when we first moved in. I'm not sure they wanted to be friends. We were an anomaly, like a sloth at the zoo.

It took us over an hour to walk around the block.

We both showered and changed for bed. The rest of the night turned out to be the most relaxing evening I'd had since the entire serial killer ordeal began.

Amy and I were at the Medical Examiner's office by eight the next morning. A doctor I didn't know stood over an autopsy table examining a body and talking quietly into a recorder. "Is this your guy?" he said without looking up.

"No," I said. "We came to speak to doctor Willis."

"I'm afraid you made a wasted trip. I guess you haven't heard the news."

We both took a step closer to the table. "What news?" I asked.

"Mrs. Willis died last night. She took her own life."

"How?" Amy asked.

"Dane, Mr. Willis, hurt his back some months back. The doctor told him to take some time off, rest and stay off his feet. I don't know how well you know him, but we all knew he wouldn't take any time off. He worked like a man possessed.

"Ever since his daughter was killed, he spent all of his time here."

I stopped listening after the sentence, *after his daughter was killed.* "Was she in an accident?"

He stopped what he was doing and looked straight at us. "No, she was killed by that maniac John Michael Malloy. The man who decided if you were unhappy you needed to die. He must have judged her unhappy, because he shot her in the back of the head.

"Jeez, I guess that's been about thirty years ago now."

Amy had the manilla envelope Dr. Willis gave us a week or so before. She took out the list of victims and read through it. She isn't on this list."

"She was married," he said. "Let me think a minute. I'll come up with the name." He stood still and silent. I could nearly see the smoke come out of the top of his head he concentrated so long. "Dana Lamb," he finally said.

Amy said, "We have a Mary D. Lamb, age twenty-three."

"That's her," the doctor said. "Mary Dana Lamb, they called her Dana."

"He never mentioned it," I said. "He knew we were investigating the murders but he didn't tell us."

"Doctor, I'm afraid I don't know your name."

"I guess I should have introduced myself. Samuel Branner. I most usually work in Kansas City. Dane and I graduated from medical school together. I don't have any family left. No one knows how long Dane, Dr. Willis will be out. I volunteered to cover his shifts."

I couldn't think of anything else to ask. Apparently, neither did Amy. She stood next to me and looked like she would fall over any minute. "Thanks for your help," I said. "I'm sure we'll see you again."

We turned and left the suite before he had a chance to say another word.

When we got back into the Range Rover, Amy said, "Guess we've been investigating the wrong people. I wonder why he did it. I don't wonder why he killed the killer, but I don't understand why he went to all the trouble to get rid of every juror.

"Thirty years is a long time. If they were going to talk, it would have been long before now."

Amy stared out the windshield. "I don't know how I'd feel if someone killed my child, but I know he or she wouldn't live long. Even if I knew I'd go to jail for killing whoever it was."

"Let's go back to the office and do a deep dive into Dr. Willis' past. I have a gut feeling he is our killer."

"Why do you think he tried to kill us?" she asked.

"I'm not sure he did. He would have finished the task if it was what he wanted. Someone who has killed as many people as he, should be very proficient at it."

It took us a few hours but we found a volume of information about Dane Allen Willis. He went to college at Truman State, which in his time was called Northeastern Missouri State. He graduated from medical school at St. Louis University School of Medicine. He did his residence at Barnes and Jewish Hospitals.

"Where do you think he got the money to pay off the jury? Who drove the limo and who came up with Enuf's Enuf?" Amy asked.

"I found out he married Missy Shackelford, heir to the Shackelford fortune."

"I'm not familiar," Amy said. "Remember, I'm not from here."

"They are an old St. Louis family. They owned

property all over the area. As the city grew, they began to sell large parcels to the big companies and to the government. According to this article I'm reading, she has, well had, over six billion dollars in net worth.

"More than enough to pay off the jury, the judge and anyone else who stood in the way. I believe the only unanswered questions is; why did he kill everyone now, after all of these years?"

I looked at my watch. "It'll have to wait. Dr. Willis isn't going anywhere. I promised Ryan I'd go with him to a reception for a retiring business owner who had done business with him for years."

Amy smiled. "I got a message from Nathan earlier. Let me read it to you. *"Hi, I don't know if you remember me or not. I'm your loving husband who has been trying to get an evening alone with you for weeks. What do you say? How about a 24 hour staycation, me, you , Digger and Sally? I'll be waiting for your answer."*

We both laughed. "I guess you need to head home. Sounds to me like an invitation you can't and wouldn't want to ignore."

Neither one of us moved. I finally said, "We both know that's a pipe dream. The only way we will see our guys tonight are if they are a part of the raid on Dr. Willis' house.

"After all this hard work, I don't want to give him a chance to slip away."

Amy shook her head. "I know, but a gal has to have a fantasy once in a while. I am going home. I want to tell Nathan, in person what is going on. I'll meet you back here—" Amy looked at her phone to see the time— "at 7:30. And remind me we are never going to

take another case for the St. Louis Police."
    "Or any other police department," I added.

CHAPTER 34

Once Amy and the dogs were gone, I went out in the backyard with Chili and Axel. The weather had turned cold. I knew the warm days would be few and far between until at least March. They both did their business and ran back through the doggy door.

I glanced at the clock, five-fifteen. I needed a moment or two to myself before what I knew would be a long, loud and emotional night.

Dr. Dane Willis had been a part of my life for years. I saw him more in the years I spent in homicide. Since I had opened the agency, we'd only had to use his services three or four times.

He never seemed to change. He stood about five-feet six, had a slight build and his head only had hair from ear to ear, in a strip about 2 inches wide. A slight man, he couldn't have tipped the scale at more than one-forty. I remember thinking how strong he was for his size. His strength came, most likely from moving, turning and working with the dead weight of the corpses he had to move.

I'd always had a soft spot for him. Still, the thought of him killing twelve people in cold blood sent chills through my body. Once I resigned my mind to what would happen to the good doctor, I called Roger Simon.

"Roger, this is Kate. We have identified the killer."

"You have?"

"Anyone I've heard of before?"

I took a deep breath, "Dr. Willis."

"You're kidding. Dane Willis wouldn't hurt a fly. And who chauffeured him around in that limo and never told a soul? Are you telling me there were two crazy people involved in this?"

"Yes. We think it was his wife who helped him. I don't know what went wrong, but we don't think she committed suicide last night. We believe he killed her."

"Jeez, Kate. Do you hear yourself? We've all known and worked with Dane for years. I've never even heard him raise his voice."

"I need to get ready. Trust me Roger, we're right. He paid off the judge and each and every juror 30 years ago. What we don't know is what happened now, thirty years later, to make him want to kill them off.

"Have a SWAT team and at least six patrolmen at 2929 Everly Rd. Tell them to stay away from the house. We don't want him to be aware of us."

"Okay, will do. See you there."

Ryan came into the kitchen. "You don't look ready to go to a formal dinner."

I walked over and gave him a big hug. "I have good news and bad."

He gently pushed me back to arm's length and looked me straight in the eye. "I'll take the bad news first. It will give me something to look forward to."

I gave him my best smile. "I can't go with you tonight."

He smiled back at me and took his hands off my shoulders. "I might need a beer for this. Want something?"

Ryan went toward the refrigerator. He took out a beer, took the lid off a wine bottle, and offered me a generous glass. He guided me toward the couch. I sat the wine on the table without tasting it. "Are you going to tell me the good news," he asked.

I held my glass up to tap it to his beer bottle. "We know who the killer is, and I think we know who drove the limo. We are putting together a SWAT team to pick him up tonight."

He took a long swig of his beer. "I guess that trumps a formal dinner with some stuffy business people."

I turned to face him. "Dr. Dane Willis."

"The medical examiner?"

"One in the same," I said. "We think his wife drove the limo. She turned up dead last night. He called it in as a suicide. We don't believes it."

He finished his beer. "Believe me, I have a thousand questions. I need to be at the restaurant within the hour and I need a shower. I expect to get the entire story out of you later. I reached up to kiss him and he kissed me back. "Have a good time. Look at it this way: My work with the police department is over. Amy and I have so many requests in our emails, we could pick and choose our jobs for the next year."

He kissed me one more time. "Tell me you will have on a bullet proof vest tonight."

"I promise," I said. "I will be toward the back of the

detail anyway. We have that SWAT team going with us. I will see you later. Have a good time."

"The most difficult chore of the evening is to make up a reasonable excuse about where you are. I am certainly not going to say my wife is arresting a serial killer."

CHAPTER 35

I picked Amy up on my way to the scene. "Do you think Dr. Willis will give up without a fight?" she asked.

"I answered her with a question. "What do you think?"

"Honestly, I think his wife grew a conscience. She told him to stop or she would tell. I believe it's why they ditched the limousine and the entire act. She dropped out of the killing.

"He finished the rest of the people he wanted to kill by himself. I believe when she found out he didn't stop, she threatened to rat him out, so he killed her."

I said, "I'm glad we don't have to prove it."

"Not our job. Once we catch them, we are out of it."

I laughed, "Except for a mountain of paperwork."

When we arrived, the SWAT team was out of their vehicles. Roger and two detectives stood near them. I hoped we hadn't kept them waiting. According to the time on my phone, we were exactly on time.

Roger and the detectives walked toward us. "Ladies, this is your parade. How do you want to proceed?"

I answered, "Send two men to cover the back door. One at the outside garage door and the rest with us. Bring the ram. By now, Willis is a seasoned killer. I don't want anyone to get hurt."

The troops began to scatter. Amy and I took the lead. When I reached the front door, I barely touched it and it opened. All of the lights were off.

Inside felt like a tomb. The crisp air didn't smell fresh. The climate in the room sent a chill through me. Amy and I both had our guns drawn. Someone behind us shined a spotlight around the room in a back and forth motion.

Dr. Willis sat in an easy chair in front of a window on the far side of the room. I didn't need a light to let me know he was dead. His head slumped to one side. A large syringe stuck in his neck with a small line of blood that ran down to his shirt.

Five minutes later the place swarmed with police and CSI officials. Roger called the Medical Examiner from Edwardsville, Illinois. He agreed to come to the scene. We had the second man from our group, but Roger didn't think it was fair to have the man do an autopsy on his friend and co-worker of twenty some years.

Amy and I were on our way to the second floor of the residence. "How do you think it got this far along?"

I said, "Sometimes a person does something they think will solve a problem when, in reality, it compounds the matter and it grows like it has a body and mind of its own.

"I just hope there is an explanation in this house or

in Dr. Willis' office which explains why."

Upstairs consisted of five rooms. The master bedroom with its vaulted ceiling and bathroom bigger than my house took up a major part of it. Three more bedrooms broke off from the hallway. The beds were made, the rooms tastefully decorated. Dust floated through the light as we opened each door.

In what looked like a large hall closet, we found an office. The furnishings consisted of a large desk pushed up against the back wall and so many file cabinets we could hardly turn around.

The desktop looked clean and dusted except for a manila folder in the middle of it. The address read, To Whom It May Concern. Amy and I each slipped on a pair of rubber gloves and I picked it up. We took it downstairs and sat at the kitchen table before we opened it.

It said;

In June of 1969, my lovely wife and I created a baby girl. Her name, Dana Willis. Dana was everything a parent could want in a child. She married a medical student. She married him at age 24 and became Mrs. Daniel Lamb.

A year later as she walked home from the library, she was unlucky enough to run into one, James Michael Malloy. Not only did he shoot her and slit her throat, but he beat her so badly her own father didn't recognize her when he began her autopsy.

The feeling I had when I opened her shirt and saw a birthmark in the shape of a star on her left breast was one I can't begin to relate to another human.

Dana was his seventh victim.

Her mother could not cope, nor could her husband.

He killed himself six months later. My wife has tried unsuccessfully several times over the years to commit suicide.

I came up with the idea to buy a jury and a judge so they would acquit the man. I would let my wife kill him and perhaps help ease her burden.

The first thing Malloy did was to buy a one way ticket out of town. My wife and I waited for him outside his hotel and when he got close enough, she shot him six times.

It didn't make her feel any better. It only added one more item to her depressed mind.

The men and women we paid off from the jury all began to live out their dream lives. Minnie could not help but follow each one. As the years passed, she became obsessed with their lives.

I believe I became as sick and obsessed with their lives as my wife did.

I could only come up with one solution. You know about it.

In the end, Minnie went mad and shot herself. Knowing the justice department as I do, I made the decision to end my life and end this nightmare.

Dane William Willis, M.D.

"Unbelievable," I said. "How could anyone think they could have a murder and conspiracy involving so many people and pull it off? In my experience, the only time you can truly get by with a crime is if you commit it alone in the bathroom or a closet with the door locked. Then it is still iffy that you might get by with it."

"No kidding," Amy said. "I wish he would have said

more. Maybe I'm sorry, thirty years ago I made a horrible mistake and instead of trying to live a better life to make up for it, he compounded it.

"Before you correct me, I know he could never make up for it, but why kill more."

"It is called insanity. I don't know if we will ever find out, but I know in my heart his wife was the driver," I said.

Roger called from downstairs. As we walked down he leaned against the stair rail talking to a man I didn't recognize. "Mr. Rains, this is Kate Nash and her partner, Amy Perkin. They are the reason this case is solved."

I couldn't see until he looked up, but he had to have been eighty years old. "Would you ladies sit with me in the den. I have a story to tell you."

We glanced at one another and followed him. The room looked like something out of Architectural Digest. Glass shelves lined the walls, the end tables and a coffee table with a dolphin etched in its glass top.

Mr. Rains began the conversation. "Dane Willis confided in me as his life unfolded. On his death, I am free to break my oath."

"I'm sorry, Mr. Rains, are you a priest?" I asked.

"No, I am Dane's neighbor. I caught him one night dressed like a woman."

Amy said, "You knew he was killing person after person and you didn't tell anyone?"

"That is correct," he said. "Are you going to arrest me?"

"It isn't up to me. I'm going to read you your rights and leave the decision to someone else. Tell us your story."

"I'd be glad too, and I'm not afraid of going to prison. I am ninety-three years old. I doubt I'll be around that much longer."

"Dane is the best friend I've ever had. I had an inkling of what he was doing when the serial killer got off scot-free. Dane spent all of his time trailing the man. When he found out he had a ticket out of town, he took Minnie with him, and after Doc subdued him, he let her shoot the man."

"You have lived with this for all of those years?" Amy asked.

"Detective Perkin, it wasn't for me to judge. You never met Dana. She had the world by it's tail and would have been a success, not the victim of a filthy man because he had judged her to be an unhappy person. I never saw a happier, more content young lady than their girl. I held her at the hospital when she was born."

"I'm not sure I might not have felt the same way." He reached into his pocket, and handed me a piece of paper. "This is a trust Dane gave me to execute. He knew you were about to catch him. He said he even went so far as to shoot at you near your home to scare you off."

"This leaves the ten billion dollar estate. He and his wife left to those he felt he wronged. He wants it split between the kids, grandkids, and wives or husbands of those he killed."

"How did he end up with ten billion dollars?"

"His wife inherited money. I doubt they spent any of the money once Dana was murdered."

"Every decision the doc made only worsened the situation. Paying off a judge, a jury and killing the defendant. Why they didn't get to the bottom of it right then, I don't know."

"Then all of the jurors were magically wealthy. Then the jurors began to die. Each one murdered. It was so long ago, no one remembered."

"Had you not been put on the case; I believe Minnie would have still killed herself. One can only grieve for so long. She never got any better. The grief didn't subside for as much as a day.

"Dane became more strange every year. He had a plan to kill them all, believing if his wife knew those families were no longer happy, she could begin to heal."

"I tried to tell him, if she didn't heal any in thirty-years, she never would."

Amy and I stood. "Mr. Rains, I'm afraid we will have to take you in for aiding and abetting a killer. Like I said, whether you are charged is not up to us. Plus, geez, who knows what they will come up with." I handed him over to a uniformed police officer. "Take this gentleman downtown and book him. No need to handcuff him. He'll go willingly." I looked at the old man. "Won't you, sir?"

He reached for the trust that laid on the table between us. "We'll keep that," Amy said as she picked it up.

CHAPTER 36

As we left the scene, I took the envelope from Amy and stuck it in front of my gun at the small of the back and pulled my jacket over it. I'd been holding back, as always, trying to figure out why so many people had to die for the happiness of one person. I hoped the trust would help me reconcile the deaths of so many people.

Each and every time I closed a murder case, I went back to the one that changed my life.

I had to leave St. Louis Homicide, where I spent ten years solving murders in the city. We were asked to help with a case where the body was found on a small island in the Mississippi River.

A jurisdictional war was about to break out between the Illinois authorities and us because the island, no more than an acre, sat in the middle of the river. To me, any dead body I didn't have to deal with, I could joyfully give up.

To solve the problem, my partner, Roger Simon, and I were sent to meet the Illinois authorities at the scene. Bile rose to my throat as we approached the tiny boat. My husband, Michael, and his brother had gone fishing three days before. They were due home the next day. Their boat was the first thing I observed when we arrived.

Michael, my beautiful Michael, the love of my life, lay dead with a bullet hole to the back of his head, execution style. His brother sat next to him sobbing uncontrollably. He'd taken the boat to a small town on the Illinois side of the river to pick up beer and charcoal. When he came back, he found his brother dead.

He couldn't get a signal on his phone so he flagged down a passing boat. They called the Coast Guard for him.

Since the time I saw Michael dead, I had too much empathy for the survivors of these horrendous crimes to be effective as a detective.

I quit.

I love Ryan Mead, with all my heart. It took me a long time to put Michael in a special place in my heart and go ahead with my life. The problem was, every time I saw, or had to deal with a murderer, I faced it again. Many months and several deaths later, I found out who killed Michael.

Amy and I had every intention of not opening the trust until we reached the office. We made it two blocks before I pulled over, shut off the engine and turned on the car's interior lights.

Of course, it began: To Whom It May Concern, but the next four paragraphs were written by Dr. Willis to try and rationalize all he'd done.

He bribed all the jurors because he, in his obviously

twisted mind, thought if Dana's mother could personally kill the man, she could find a way to go on. As the years went by, she became obsessed with the lives of the people on the jury who were bribed.

They got married, had children, were joyous, sad, some died, but nothing brought peace to her.

As a solution to the problem, I began killing the jurors one by one. Nothing helped. Finally, I knew the only way to put my wife at peace was to let her die.

When you read this, I will also be dead. I work with the deceased all day. I know how it destroys families. In restitution, I leave my entire estate to the heirs of the people I killed.

I hope God will have mercy on my soul.

We sat in silence. This case only went from bad to worse. In the twisted mind of a killer is the false assumption taking a life can be forgiven.

In my experience as a cop and an observer of human nature, I can tell you, there is no going back.

I looked toward Amy, who hadn't said a word since I parked the car. A tear ran down her cheek.

We knew something Dane Willis did not. All the money in the world could not erase the death of a loved one, especially at the hand of another.

I agreed with one thing about the case. One murder is enough.

~ ~ ~ ~ ~

The authorities, from the top brass down to Roger Simon were glad to have the case solved. Amy and I were happy to get our lives back.

No one seemed to care about Clara Clark. Did she

drive the limo, or did Missy Willis?

I knew Amy and I would both be bugged about it until we figured it out.

There were reports upon reports to type up and file. Every day we worked to close the door on Dr. Willis' case the more I remembered all the bull I had to go through when I was a cop.

Amy and I talked about Clara Clark more than once. Who she was, why she helped Dr. Willis and where she was now. We also talked about whether we should include her in our reports.

We decided, yes, and I didn't have a good feeling about her.

I knew we would run into her again one day.

ABOUT THE AUTHOR

Susan Keene won her first literary award at the age of sixteen. Marriage, children, and the responsibilities attached to them, forced her to put her dream of being a full-time writer on the back burner.

Over the years, she wrote articles for newspapers and magazines. You might have read some of her work in the airline magazines as you fly from one place to another.

For the last ten plus years, Susan has achieved her goal to write fulltime as an award-winning author.

You'll often find Susan speaking at conferences, book clubs and writer's organizations. She also teaches a class on her craft, How to Write a Cozy Mystery. It has spurred many a wannabe writer to take the chance and write a Cozy.

Susan lives on a farm in the beautiful Ozarks where she writes her books in a little blue cottage, accompanied by her many pets. Her greatest joys are her grandchildren and her daughter. Susan's hobbies are reading, cooking, metal detecting, magnet fishing and hanging with her friends.

She loves hearing from her fans.

WEDDING CAKE MURDER

CHAPTER ONE

As I opened the door to the restaurant I heard my mother's voice echo from the kitchen. She barked orders like a drill sergeant. No telling what she was up to. She never set out to raise havoc, yet catastrophe followed her around like a puppy dog.

To stop her tirade, I walked up, stood behind her, and tapped her lightly on the shoulder. She jumped forward, turned around and put her hand over her heart. "Arizona Summers, you're going to be the death of me yet."

"Mom what's going on? Why are you yelling at the kitchen staff? And in a voice, I might add, that could shatter crystal."

She said nothing but stepped aside so I could enter the belly of the café where the food was prepared. I looked around. "My goodness, James, why's all the bread dough still unbaked? We open in less than an hour."

My mother, who now stood behind me, found her tongue and answered before the chef had a chance to speak. "We were running late. I told the cooks to dispense with the bread and to use the ovens for the desserts."

James looked my way and shrugged his shoulders.

With my hands on my hips I turned to face her. To

deal with my mother could be compared to tackling a blizzard without a coat and hat.

I looked at her and stifled a laugh. She wore a teal green tank covered with a long cardigan in pale yellow. From the waist down, she wore only her underwear. Due to the length of her top I doubt the staff noticed.

"Mother, there's an order in which we do things around here. You taught it to me when I was a child and you went over it enough times I repeated it in my sleep.

"We fix the main dishes, sides, salads and the bread. Once those are finished we bake the pies and cakes. People eat dessert last. We have more time to prepare those than the main courses. I know you haven't forgotten so what's up?"

Every day it became clearer why the younger generation took over the cafe when their parent reached her seventy-fifth birthday. I was the fifth generation of Summers to run Moonstone Lake's favorite dining spot.

Some days I wondered if I would survive Emma's interference. In my childhood I called her Emma to catch her attention. Like many busy moms she could block out my constant interruptions.

Sunday brunch took my full attention. I asked her if I could speak to her in the hall. Once we were face to face I said, "I know you like to be in charge but it doesn't work anymore. Please go home and get dressed if you want to mingle with the diners. I suggest you don't do it in your under pants."

She looked down, raised her sweater a little and said, "I'm dressed."

"And you look very nice; from the waist up. I believe skirt or slacks would set off your lovely outfit better than your granny panties."

She turned on her heel and lumbered out the side door. Too many years of restaurant food, mostly desserts, had taken its toll. She looked back to get in the last word. "I don't wear granny panties."

I watched until she disappeared.

Once I heard the door close I returned to the kitchen to try to salvage the day. James walked over to stand beside me. "I'm sorry Ary. I never know what to say to her."

"I know, James, it isn't your fault. I'll call the Amazin' Glazin' and see if they can spare any bread. Meanwhile put as many loaves as possible in the ovens."

The bakery offered us fifteen loaves. I walked across the Boardwalk to pick them up.

Dottie Wittmore had run the Amazin' Glazin' Bakery for as long as I could remember. The aroma of pastries and breads wafted out to the sidewalk. I smelled chocolate, peppermint and fresh rye. I smiled to myself. You'd think the smells would mingle and give off a toxic fume. Somehow they stayed separate. I lingered outside to savor the aroma.

The bakery was full. Both cash registers had lines at least six customers deep. I waved at Dottie and stood to the side, out of the way, until she had time for me.

A young couple sat in the back under an arch in an area decorated like a wedding dome. Many brides and grooms sat there over the years to design their wedding cakes.

Stacy Young and a handsome young man were seated in two of the four chairs arranged around a small heart-shaped table. He had his hand on hers and smiled every time she spoke. What caught my eye were the two women who sat with them. I knew one to be Stacy's mother, Denise. She and I frequented the same book club. The other lady looked out of place in her purple feathered hat, long black coat, brown orthopedic shoes and white gloves.

I watched the four of them. The lady in black threw a hissy-fit. I couldn't hear the conversation but her gestures and tones were unmistakable. I knew the other three and the cake designer had to have been horrified when the bakery became dead silent and the patrons all turned to stare at them.

The woman stood and in a voice the entire shop could hear yelled. "I knew this wedding would be a joke. I should have insisted the ceremony and reception be held in Boston. There's no way this man is a professional cake designer, the church only holds a hundred guests and the reception is at a diner whose claim to fame is a Sunday Brunch."

She looked down at her son. I half expected venom to spurt from her mouth. "And I don't care what your reasoning. I refuse to allow you to have a gray armadillo-shaped groom's cake with gray icing and red cream filling."

As she finished her rude comments I thought of my mother. She had become an instant angel in my mind.

I put my hand over my mouth to stifle a laugh as I visualized the armadillo cake and its gooey filling. On her way out the woman knocked into my skinny frame which caused me to hit the wall behind me. Her feathered hat sailed off her head. No one moved. She reached down picked it up slammed it down cockeyed on her head and stormed toward the door.

She didn't offer an apology. I said an aggravated

"Excuse me," as she left. She turned and glared.

Dottie called me to the counter. Fifteen loaves of various varieties of bread stuck out of two huge brown paper bags. "I thought you baked your own bread. Everything all right over there?"

"Yes we lost track of time today." I nodded toward Michael, the cake designer. "What just happened?"

"The groom's mother's a witch. I'm being kind. They've been here three separate times to pick out a cake. The wedding is in less than six weeks. His mother doesn't like anything. I swear, if someone gave her a million dollars she wouldn't take it because it would be the wrong shade of green.

"I told Michael not to put up with it. We don't need business that bad. I wonder how his mother would get along with Suzie, who ices the cakes at Discount Grocery. They're the next closest thing to a bakery within thirty-miles.

"Mike said he hated to send them away. He and Stacy became close friends when she worked here during her college breaks."

I took the bag she handed me. "Who's the groom? He's a real cutie; he obviously has the patience of a saint if he sat through that with his mother more than once."

"Stacy introduced him as Dillon Freedman. We don't have to guess where he's from; his mother has screamed it enough. Can you imagine comparing our little town of twenty-two hundred to Boston and its hundreds of thousands of people?"

I turned toward the door. "It takes all kinds. I'd better get back. We open in ten minutes. What do I owe you?"

"Oh honey, I'll bill you. You run along."

On the way back I thought about Stacy's mom. The bride's family customarily paid for most of a wedding. Mrs. Young called a few weeks earlier to schedule a time to meet and select the food for the reception. I got a chill at the thought of having to deal with the groom's mother. At least I had seen her in action and knew what to expect.

The kitchen had settled down by the time I got back. James and one of the line cooks sliced the bread I brought with me.

The waiters and waitresses were lined up for the little talk I had with the entire crew as often as I could before we opened. I likened it to the stewardess who stands in the front of the plane to explain to the passengers how to survive a crash. They were there and attentive but I knew if push came to shove we'd all go down with the ship.

They needed a reminder more than ever on brunch day. "Everyone looks neat and clean, thank you. Remember; keep water glasses, coffee cups, soft drinks and tea glasses full.

"Remove plates from the tables in a timely manner. You don't have to put up with cursing, abuse, touching or general orneriness. Do not handle it yourself. Keep smiling and come get me. I'll take care of it. Mitch and Sara, take section 1, Stan and April 2, Mark and Benny, 3 and Jan and Patty, 4. Good luck out there."

I didn't actually view the dining room as a war zone. We rarely had any problems.

Mom and the bread situation slowed me down. I hadn't changed out of my running clothes. I yelled at my best friend and aunt who stood at the hostess podium. "Sandy, I'll be back in five minutes."

As I went home to change I thought about my Aunt Sandy and how expertly she directed traffic every Sunday. If left unattended and allowed to seat themselves, some customers acted like a herd of cows who tried to get through a narrow gate at the same time. If it were not for my mother's youngest sister, there would be a weekly stampede nearly as dangerous as the Running of the Bulls in Pamplona.

People pushed and shoved to commandeer a seat as close to the buffet table as possible. To some it equated to tickets on the fifty-yard line at a professional football game. A seat near the buffet line became prime real estate on Sundays. The closer people were seated to the food the less time they stood and line in more time they had to eat.

I hated the *all you can eat* concept. Too many diners took it as a challenge. I preferred *all you care to eat.*

www.ingramcontent.com/pod-product-compliance
Lightning Source LLC
Chambersburg PA
CBHW061157170626
46809CB00003B/1136